C000015526

D.H. LAWRENCE

Jimmy and the Desperate Woman & other stories

Selected by GILES GORDON

BLOOMSBURY CLASSICS

This collection first published 1996
Bloomsbury Publishing Plc, 2 Soho Square, London W1V 6HB

A CIP catalogue record for this book is available from the British Library

ISBN 0 7475 2431 9

10 9 8 7 6 5 4 3 2 1

Jacket design by Jeff Fisher
Typeset by Hewer Text Composition Services, Edinburgh
Printed by St Edmundsbury Press, Suffolk

Acknowledgements

The Prussian Officer and Other Stories – including the title story, 'Second-Best' and 'A Sick Collier' – was Lawrence's first published collection of stories (Duckworth, 1914). 'A Sick Collier' was written in 1912, 'The Prussian Officer' in its first version in 1913, and 'Second-Best' in 1913 or 1914.

The Woman Who Rode Away and other Stories – including the title story, 'Jimmy and the Desperate Woman' and 'Sun' – was first published by Martin Secker in 1928. 'Jimmy and the Desperate Woman' was written in 1924, 'The Woman Who Rode Away' was first published in 1925, and 'Sun' written in 1925.

The copyright line in the Penguin edition of *The Prussian Officer and Other Stories* (first published by CUP 1983; in Penguin Books 1995) reads: copyright © the Estate of Frieda Lawrence Ravagli, 1983. There is no copyright line in the Penguin (first published 1950) *The Woman Who Rode Away and Other Stories*.

Contents

A Sick Collier

She was too good for him, everybody said. Yet still she did not regret marrying him. He had come courting her when he was only nineteen, and she twenty. He was in build what they call a tight little fellow: short, dark, with a warm colour, and that upright set of the head and chest, that flaunting way in movement recalling a mating bird, which denote a body taut and compact with life. Being a good worker, he had earned decent money in the mine, and, having a good home, had saved a little.

She was a cook at 'Uplands', a tall, fair girl, very quiet. Having seen her walk down the street, Horsepool had followed her from a distance. He was taken with her, he did not drink, and he was not lazy. So, although he seemed a bit simple, without much intelligence, but having a sort of physical brightness, she considered, and accepted him.

When they were married they went to live in Scargill Street, in a highly respectable six-roomed house which they had furnished between them.

The street was built up the side of a long, steep hill. It was narrow and rather tunnel-like. Nevertheless, the back looked out over the adjoining pasture, across a wide valley of fields and woods, in the bottom of which the mine lay snugly.

He made himself gaffer in his own house. She was unacquainted with a collier's mode of life. They were married on a Saturday. On the Sunday night, he said:

'Set th' table for my breakfast, an' put my pit-things afront o' th' fire. I s'll be gettin' up at ha'ef pas' five. Tha nedna shift thy-sen not till when ter likes.'

He showed her how to put a newspaper on the table for a cloth. When she demurred:

'I want none o' your white cloths i' th' mornin'. I like ter be able to slobber if I feel like it,' he said.

He put before the fire his moleskin trousers, a clean singlet, or sleeveless vest of thick flannel, a pair of stockings and his pit boots, arranging them all to be warm and ready for morning.

'Now tha sees. That wants doin' ivery night.'

Punctually at half-past five, he left her, without any form of leave-taking, going downstairs in his shirt.

When he arrived home at four o'clock in the afternoon, his dinner was ready to be dished up. She was startled when he came in, a short, sturdy figure, with a face indescribably black and streaked. She stood before the fire in her white blouse and white apron, a fair girl, the picture of beautiful cleanliness. He 'clommaxed' in, in his heavy boots.

'Well how 'as ter gone on?' he asked.

'I was ready for you to come home,' she replied tenderly. In his black face, the whites of his brown eyes flashed at her.

'An' I wor ready for commin',' he said.

He planked his tin bottle and snap-bag on the dresser, took off his coat and scarf and waistcoat, dragged his armchair nearer the fire, and sat down.

'Let's ha'e a bit o' dinner, then – I'm about clammed,' he said.

'Aren't you goin' to wash yourself first?'

'What am I to wesh my-sen for?'

'Well, you can't eat your dinner—'

'Oh, strike a daisy Missis! Dunna I eat my snap i' th' pit' wi'out weshin'? – Forced to.'

She served the dinner, and sat opposite him. His small, bullet head was quite black, save for the whites of his eyes and his scarlet lips. It gave her a queer sensation to see him open his red mouth, and bare his white teeth, as he ate. His arms and hands were mottled black; his bare, strong neck got a little fairer as it settled towards his shoulders, reassuring her. There was the faint indescribable odour of the pit in the room, an odour of damp, exhausted air.

'Why is your vest so black on the shoulders?' she asked.

'My singlet? That's wi' th' watter droppin' on us from th' roof. This is a dry un as I put on afore I

come up. They ha'e gre't clothes-'osses, an' as we
change us things we put 'em on theer ter dry.'

When he washed himself, kneeling on the
hearth rug stripped to the waist, she felt afraid of
him again. He was so muscular, he seemed so
intent on what he was doing, so intensely himself,
like a vigorous animal. And as he stood wiping
himself, with his naked breast towards her, she felt
rather sick, seeing his thick arms bulge their
muscles.

They were nevertheless very happy. He was at
a great pitch of pride because of her. The men in
the pit might chaff him, they might try to entice
him away, but nothing could reduce his self-
assured pride because of her, nothing could
unsettle his almost infantile satisfaction. In the
evening he sat in his armchair chattering to her, or
listening as she read the newspaper to him. When
it was fine, he would go into the street, squat on
his heels as colliers do, with his back against the
wall of his parlour, and call to the passers by, in
greeting, one after another. If no one were
passing, he was content just to squat and smoke,
having such a fund of sufficiency and satisfaction
in his heart. He was well married.

They had not been wed a year when all Brent
and Wellwood's men came out on strike. Willy
was in the Union, so with a pinch they scrambled
through. The furniture was not all paid for, and
other debts were incurred. She worried and
contrived, he left it to her. But he was a good
husband; he gave her all he had.

The men were out fifteen weeks. They had
been back just over a year when Willy had an
accident in the mine, tearing his bladder. At the
pit-head, the doctor talked of the hospital. Losing
his head entirely, the young collier raved like a
madman, what with pain and fear of hospital.

'Tha s'llt go whoam, Willy, tha s'llt go
whoam,' the deputy said.

A lad warned the wife to have the bed ready.
Without speaking or hesitating, she prepared.
But when the ambulance came, and she heard
him shout with pain at being moved, she was
afraid lest she should sink down. They carried
him in.

'Yo' should 'a had a bed i' th' parlour, Missis,'
said the deputy, 'then we shouldna ha' had to
hawkse 'im upstairs, an' it 'ud 'a saved your legs.'

But it was too late now. They got him upstairs.

'They let me lie, Lucy,' he was crying, 'they let
me lie two mortal hours on th' sleck, afore they
took me outer th' stall. Th' peen, Lucy, th' peen,
Oh, Lucy, th' peen, th' peen!'

'I know th' pain's bad, Willy, I know. But you
must try an' bear it a bit.'

'Tha munna carry on in that form, lad, thy
Missis'll niver be able ter stan' it,' said the deputy.

'I canna 'elp it, it's th' peen, it's th' peen,' he
cried again. He had never been ill in his life.
When he had had a smashed finger, he could look
at the wound. But this pain came from inside, and
terrified him.

At last he was soothed and exhausted.

It was some time before she could undress him and wash him. He would let no other woman do for him, having that savage modesty usual in such men.

For six weeks he was in bed, suffering much pain. The doctors were not quite sure what was the matter with him, and scarcely knew what to do. He could eat, he did not lose flesh, nor strength, yet the pain continued, and he could hardly walk at all.

In the sixth week, the men came out in the national strike. He would get up quite early in the morning, and sit by the window. On Wednesday, the second week of the strike, he sat gazing out on the street as usual, a bullet headed young man, still vigorous looking, but with a peculiar expression of hunted fear in his face.

'Lucy,' he called, 'Lucy!'

She, pale and worn, ran upstairs at his bidding.

'Gi'e me a han'kercher,' he said.

'Why, you've got one,' she replied, coming near.

'Tha nedna touch me,' he cried. Feeling in his pocket, he produced a white handkerchief.

'I non want a white un, gi'e me a red un,' he said.

'An' if anybody comes to see you,' she answered, giving him a red handkerchief.

'Besides,' she continued, 'you needn't ha' brought me upstairs for that.'

'I b'lieve th' peen's commin' on again,' he said, with a little horror in his voice.

'It isn't, you know it isn't,' she replied. 'The doctor says you imagine it's there when it isn't.'

'Canna I feel what's inside me!' he shouted.

'There's a traction engine coming down-hill,' she said. 'That'll scatter them – I'll just go an' finish your pudding.'

She left him. The traction engine went by, shaking the houses. Then the street was quiet, save for the men. A gang of youths from fifteen to twenty-five years old were playing marbles in the middle of the road. Other little groups of men were playing on the pavement. The street was gloomy. Willy could hear the endless calling and shouting of men's voices.

'Tha 'rt skinchin'!'

'I arena!'

– 'Come 'ere with that blood-alley.'

'Swop us four for 't.'

'Shonna, gie's hold on 't.'

He wanted to be out, he wanted to be playing marbles. The pain had weakened his mind, so that he hardly knew any self-control.

Presently, another gang of men lounged up the street. It was pay morning. The Union was paying the men in the Primitive Chapel. They were returning with their half sovereigns.

'Sorry!' bawled a voice, 'Sorry!'

The word is a form of address, corruption probably of 'Sirrah.' Willy started almost out of his chair.

'Sorry!' again bawled a great voice. 'Art goin' wi' me to see Notts play Villa?'

Many of the marble players started up.

'What time is it? – There's no treens, we s'll ha'e ter walk.'

The street was alive with men.

'Who's goin' ter Nottingham ter see th' match?' shouted the same big voice. A very large, tipsy man, with his cap over his eye, was calling.

'Com' on – ay, com' on!' came many voices. The street was full of the shouting of men. They split up in excited cliques and groups.

'Play up Notts,' the big man shouted.

'Plee up Notts!' shouted the youths and men. They were at kindling pitch. It only needed a shout to rouse them. Of this, the careful authorities were aware.

'I'm goin', I'm goin'!' shouted the sick man at his window.

Lucy came running upstairs.

'I'm goin' ter see Notts play Villa on th' Meadows ground,' he declared.

'You – *you* can't go. There are no trains. You can't walk nine miles.'

'I'm goin' ter see th' match,' he declared, rising.

'You know you can't – Sit down now an' be quiet.'

She put her hand on him. He shook it off.

'Leave me alone, leave me alone. It's thee as ma'es th' peen come, it's thee. I'm goin' ter Nottingham to see th' football match.'

'Sit down – folk'll hear you, and what will they think.'

'Come off'n me. Com' off. It's her, it's her as does it. Com' off.'

He seized hold of her. His little head was bristling with madness, and he was strong as a lion.

'Oh Willy!' she cried.

'It's 'er, it's 'er. Kill her,' he shouted, 'Kill her.'

'Willy, folks'll hear you.'

'Th' peen's commin' on again, I tell yer. I'll kill her for it.'

He was completely out of his mind. She struggled with him, to prevent his going to the stairs. When she escaped from him, who was shouting and raving, she beckoned to her neighbour, a girl of twenty-four, who was cleaning the window across the road.

Ethel Mellor was the daughter of a well-to-do check-weighman. She ran across in fear to Mrs Horsepool. Hearing the man raving, people were running out in the street, and listening. Ethel hurried upstairs. Everything was clean and pretty in the young home.

Willy was staggering round the room, after the slowly retreating Lucy, shouting:

'Kill 'er! Kill 'er!'

'Mr Horsepool!' cried Ethel, leaning against the bed, white as the sheets, and trembling. 'Whatever are you saying?'

'I tell yer it's 'er fault as th' pain comes on – I tell yer it is! Kill 'er – kill 'er.'

'Kill Mrs Horsepool!' cried the trembling girl. 'Why you're ever so fond of her, you know you are.'

'The peen – I ha'e such a lot o' peen – I want to kill 'er.'

He was subsiding. When he sat down, his wife collapsed in a chair, weeping noiselessly. The tears ran down Ethel's face. He sat staring out of the window; then the old, hurt look came on his face.

'What 'ave I been sayin'?' he asked, looking piteously at his wife.

'Why!' said Ethel. 'You've been carrying on something awful, saying "Kill her, kill her!" '

'Have I, Lucy?' he faltered.

'You didn't know what you was saying,' said his young wife gently but coldly.

His face puckered up. He bit his lip, then broke into tears, sobbing uncontrollably, with his face to the window.

There was no sound in the room but of three people crying bitterly, breath caught in sobs. – Suddenly Lucy put away her tears, and went over to him.

'You didn't know what you was sayin', Willy, I know you didn't. I knew you didn't, all the time. It doesn't matter, Willy. Only don't do it again.'

In a little while, when they were calmer, she went downstairs with Ethel.

'See if anybody is looking in the street,' she said.

Ethel went into the parlour and peeped through the curtains.

'Ay!' she said. 'You may back your life Lena an' Mrs Severn 'll be out gorping, and that clat-fartin' Mrs Allsop.'

'Oh, I hope they haven't heard anything! If it

gets about as he's out of his mind, they'll stop his compensation, I know they will.'

'They'd never stop his compensation for *that*,' protested Ethel.

'Well, they *have* been stopping some—'

'It'll not get about. I s'll tell nobody.'

'Oh, but if it does, whatever shall we do?—'

The Prussian Officer [Honour and Arms]

They had marched more than thirty kilometres since dawn, along the white, hot road, where occasional thickets of trees threw a moment of shade, then out into the glare again. On either hand, the valley, wide and shallow, glistered with heat; dark green patches of rye, pale young corn, fallow and meadow and black pine-woods spread in a dull, hot diagram under a glistening sky. But right in front the mountains ranged across, pale blue and very still, the snow gleaming gently out of the deep atmosphere. And towards the mountains, on and on, the regiment marched between the rye-fields and the meadows, between the scraggy fruit-trees set regularly on either side the highroad. The burnished, dark green rye threw off a suffocating heat, the mountains drew gradually nearer and more distinct. While the feet of the soldiers grew hotter, sweat ran through their hair under their helmets, and their knapsacks could burn no more in contact with their shoulders, but seemed instead to give off a cold, prickly sensation.

He walked on and on in silence, staring at the mountains ahead, that rose sheer out of the land, and stood fold behind fold, half earth, half heaven, the heaven, the barrier with slits of soft snow in the pale, bluish peaks.

He could now walk almost without pain. At the start, he had determined not to limp. It had made him sick to take the first steps, and during the first mile or so, he had compressed his breath, and the cold drops of sweat had stood on his forehead. But he had walked it off. What were they after all but bruises! He had looked at them, as he was getting up: deep bruises on the backs of his thighs. And since he had made his first step in the morning, he had been conscious of them, till now he had a tight, hot place in his chest, with suppressing the pain, and holding himself in. There seemed no air when he breathed. But he walked almost lightly.

The captain's hand had trembled in taking his coffee at dawn: his orderly saw it again. And he saw the fine figure of the captain wheeling on horseback at the farmhouse ahead, a handsome figure in pale blue uniform with facings of scarlet, and the metal gleaming on the black helmet and the sword scabbard, and dark streaks of sweat coming on the silky bay horse. The orderly felt he was connected with that figure moving so suddenly on horseback: he followed it like a shadow, mute and inevitable and damned by it. And the officer was always aware of the tramp of the company behind, the march of his orderly among the men.

The captain was a tall man of about forty, grey at the temples. He had a handsome, finely-knit figure, and was one of the best horsemen in the West. His orderly, having to rub him down, admired the amazing riding-muscles of his loins.

For the rest, the orderly scarcely noticed the officer any more than he noticed himself. It was rarely he saw his master's face: he did not look at it. The captain had reddish-brown, stiff hair, that he wore short upon his skull. His moustache also was cut short and bristly over a full, brutal mouth. His face was rather rugged, the cheeks thin. Perhaps the man was the more handsome for the deep lines in his face, the irritable tension of his brow, which gave him the look of a man who fights with life. His fair eyebrows stood bushy over light blue eyes that were always flashing with cold fire.

He was a Prussian aristocrat, haughty and overbearing. But his mother had been a Polish Countess. Having made too many gambling debts when he was young, he had ruined his prospects in the army, and remained an infantry captain. He had never married: his position did not allow it, and no woman had ever moved him to it. His time he spent riding – occasionally he rode one of his own horses at the races – and at the officers' club. Now and then he took himself a mistress. But after such an event, he returned to duty with his brow still more tense, his eyes still more hostile and irritable. With the men, however, he was merely impersonal, though a devil when roused, so that on the whole they feared him but had no great aversion from him. They accepted him as the inevitable.

To his orderly he was at first cold and just and indifferent: he did not fuss over trifles. So that his servant knew practically nothing about him, except just what orders he would give, and how he wanted them obeyed. That was quite simple. Then the change gradually came.

The orderly was a youth of about twenty-two, of medium height, and well-built. He had strong, heavy limbs, was swarthy, with a soft, black, young moustache. There was something altogether warm and young about him. He had firmly marked eyebrows over dark, expressionless eyes, that seemed never to have thought, only to have received life direct through his senses, and acted straight from instinct.

Gradually the officer had become aware of his servant's young, vigorous, unconscious presence about him. He could not get away from the sense of the youth's person, while he was in attendance. It was like a warm flame upon the older man's tense, rigid body, that had become almost unliving, fixed. There was something so free and self-contained about him, and something in the young fellow's movement, that made the officer aware of him. And this irritated the Prussian. He did not choose to be touched into life by his servant. He might easily have changed his man, but he did not. He now very rarely looked direct at his orderly, but kept his face averted, as if to avoid

seeing him. And yet as the young soldier moved
unthinking about the apartment, the elder
watched him, and would notice the movement
of his strong young shoulders under the blue
cloth, the bend of his neck. And it irritated him.
To see the soldier's young, brown, shapely
peasants' hands grasp the loaf or the winebottle
sent a flash of hate or of anger through the elder
man's blood. It was not that the youth was
clumsy: it was rather the blind, instinctive sure-
ness of movement of an unhampered young
animal that irritated the officer to such a degree.

Once, when a bottle of wine had gone over,
and the red gushed out onto the tablecloth, the
officer had started up with an oath, and his eyes,
bluey like fire, had held those of the confused
youth for a moment. It was a shock for the young
soldier. He felt something sink deeper, deeper
into his soul, where nothing had ever gone
before. It left him rather blank and wondering.
Some of his natural completeness in himself was
gone, a little uneasiness took its place. And from
that time an undiscovered feeling had held
between the two men.

Henceforward the orderly was afraid of really
meeting his master. His subconsciousness remembered those steely blue eyes and the harsh brows,
and did not intend to meet them again. So he
always stared past his master, and avoided him.
Also, in a little anxiety, he waited for the three
months to have gone, when his time would be
up. He began to feel a constraint in the captain's

presence, and the soldier even more than the officer wanted to be left alone in his neutrality as servant.

He had served the captain for more than a year, and knew his duty. This he performed easily, as if it were natural to him. The officer and his commands he took for granted, as he took the sun and the rain, and he served as a matter of course. It did not implicate him personally.

But now if he were going to be forced into a personal interchange with his master, he would be like a wild thing caught, he felt he must get away.

But the influence of the young soldier's being had penetrated through the officer's stiffened discipline, and perturbed the man in him. He, however, was a gentleman, with long fine hands and cultivated movements, and was not going to allow such a thing as the stirring of his innate self. He was a man of passionate temper, who had always kept himself suppressed. Occasionally there had been a duel, an outburst before the soldiers. He knew himself to be always on the point of breaking out. But he kept himself hard to the idea of the Service. Whereas the young soldier seemed to live out his warm, full nature, to give it off in his very movements, which had a certain zest, such as wild animals have in free movement. And this irritated the officer more and more.

In spite of himself, the captain could not regain his neutrality of feeling towards his orderly. Nor could he leave the man alone. In spite of himself, he watched him, gave him sharp orders, tried to take up as much of his time as possible. Sometimes he flew into a rage with the young soldier, and bullied him. Then the orderly shut himself off, as it were out of earshot, and waited with sullen, flushed face, for the end of the noise. The words never pierced to his intelligence, he made himself, protectively, impervious to the feelings of his master.

He had a scar on his left thumb, a deep seam going across the knuckle. The officer had long suffered from it, and wanted to do something to it. Still it was there, ugly and brutal on the young, brown hand. At last the captain's reserve gave way. One day, as the orderly was smoothing out the tablecloth, the officer pinned down his thumb with a pencil, asking:

'How did you come by that?'

The young man winced and drew back at attention.

'A wood-axe, Herr Hauptmann,' he answered.

The officer waited for further explanation. None came. The orderly went about his duties. The elder man was sullenly angry. His servant avoided him. And the next day he had to use all his will-power to avoid seeing the scarred thumb. He wanted to get hold of it and—. A hot flame ran in his blood.

He knew his servant would soon be free, and would be glad. As yet, the soldier had held himself off from the elder man. The captain grew madly irritable. He could not rest when the soldier was

away, and when he was present, he glared at him
with tormented eyes. He hated those fine black
brows over the unmeaning dark eyes, he was
infuriated by the free movement of the handsome limbs, which no military discipline could
make stiff. And he became harsh and cruelly
bullying, using contempt and satire. The young
soldier only grew more mute and expressionless.

'What cattle were you bred by, that you can't
keep straight eyes. Look me in the eyes when I
speak to you.'

And the soldier turned his dark eyes to the
other's face, but there was no sight in them: he
stared with the slightest possible cast, holding back
his sight, perceiving the blue of his master's eyes,
but receiving no look from them. And the elder
man went pale, and his reddish eyebrows
twitched. He gave his order, barrenly.

Once he flung a heavy military glove into the
young soldier's face. Then he had the satisfaction
of seeing the black eyes flare up into his own, like
a blaze when straw is thrown on a fire. And he
had laughed with a little tremor and a sneer.

But there were only two months more. The
young instinctively tried to keep himself intact: he
tried to serve the officer as if the latter were an
abstract authority, and not a man. All his instinct
was to avoid personal contact, even definite hate.
But in spite of himself the hate grew, responsive
to the officer's passion. However, he put it in the
background. When he had left the army he could
dare acknowledge it. By nature he was active, and

had many friends. He thought what amazing good fellows they were. But, without knowing it, he was alone. Now this solitariness was intensified. It would carry him through his term. But the officer seemed to be going irritably insane, and the youth was deeply frightened.

The soldier had a sweetheart, a girl from the mountains, independent and primitive. The two walked together, rather silently. He went with her, not to talk, but to have his arm round her, and for the physical contact. This eased him, made it easier for him to ignore the captain; for he could rest with her held fast against his chest. And she, in some unspoken fashion, was there for him. They loved each other.

The captain perceived it, and was mad with irritation. He kept the young man engaged all the evenings long, and took pleasure in the dark look that came on his face. Occasionally, the eyes of the two men met, those of the younger sullen and dark, doggedly unalterable, those of the elder sneering with restless contempt.

The officer tried hard not to admit the passion that had got hold of him. He would not know that his feeling for his orderly was anything but that of a man incensed by his stupid, *perverse* servant. So, keeping quite justified and conventional in his consciousness, he let the other thing run on. His nerves, however, were suffering. At last he slung the end of a belt in his servant's face. When he saw the youth start back, the pain-tears in his eyes and the blood on his mouth, he had felt at once a thrill of deep pleasure, and of shame.

But this, he acknowledged to himself was a thing he had never done before. The fellow was too exasperating. His own nerves must be going to pieces. He went away for some days with a woman.

It was a mockery of pleasure. He simply did not want the woman. But he stayed on for his time. At the end of it, he came back in an agony of irritation, torment, and misery. He rode all the evening, then came straight in to supper. His orderly was out. The officer sat with his long, fine hands lying on the table, perfectly still, and all his blood seemed to be corroding.

At last his servant entered. He watched the strong, easy young figure, the fine eyebrows, the thick black hair. In a week's time the youth had got back his old well-being. The hands of the officer twitched, and seemed to be full of mad flame. The young man stood at attention, unmoving, shut off.

The meal went in silence. But the orderly seemed eager. He made a clatter with the dishes.

'Are you in a hurry?' asked the officer, watching the intent, warm face of his servant. The other did not reply.

'Will you answer my question?' said the captain.

'Yes Sir,' replied the orderly, standing with his pile of deep army-plates. The captain waited, looked at him, then asked again:

'Are you in a hurry?'

'Yes Sir,' came the answer, that sent a flash through the listener.

'For what?'

'I was going out Sir.'

'I want you this evening.'

There was a moment's hesitation. The officer had a curious stiffness of countenance.

'Yes Sir,' replied the servant, in his throat.

'I want you tomorrow evening also – in fact you may consider your evenings occupied, unless I give you leave.'

The mouth with the young moustache set close.

'Yes Sir,' answered the orderly, loosening his lips for a moment.

He again turned to the door.

'And why have you a piece of pencil in your ear?'

The orderly hesitated, then continued on his way without answering. He set the plates in a pile outside the door, took the stump of pencil from his ear, and put it in his pocket. He had been copying a verse for his sweetheart's birthday card. He returned to finish clearing the table. The officer's eyes were dancing, he had a little, eager smile.

'Why have you a piece of pencil in your ear?' he asked.

The orderly took his hands full of dishes. His master was standing near the great green stove, a little smile on his face, his chin thrust forward. When the young soldier saw him his heart suddenly ran hot. He felt blind. Instead of answering, he turned dazedly to the door. As he was crouching to set down the dishes, he was pitched forward by a kick from behind. The pots went in a stream down the stairs, he clung to the pillar of the banisters. And as he was rising he was kicked heavily again, and again, so that he clung sickly to the post for some moments. His master had gone swiftly into the room and closed the door. The maid-servant downstairs looked up the staircase and made a mocking face at the crockery disaster.

The officer's heart was plunging. He poured himself a glass of wine, part of which he spilled on the floor, and gulped the remainder, leaning against the cool, green stove. He heard his man collecting the dishes from the stairs. Pale, as if intoxicated, he waited. The servant entered again. The captain's heart gave a pang, as of pleasure, seeing the young fellow bewildered and uncertain on his feet, with pain.

'Schöner!' he said.

The soldier was a little slower in coming to attention.

'Yes Sir!'

The youth stood before him, with pathetic young moustache, and fine eyebrows very distinct on his forehead of dark marble.

'I asked you a question.'

'Yes Sir.'

The officer's tone bit like acid.

'Why had you a pencil in your ear?'

Again the servant's heart ran hot, and he could not breathe. With dark, strained eyes, he looked at the officer, as if fascinated. And he stood there sturdily planted, unconscious. The dithering smile came into the captain's eyes, and he lifted his foot.

'I – I forgot it – Sir,' panted the soldier, his dark eyes fixed on the other man's dancing blue ones.

'What was it doing there?'

He saw the young man's breast heaving as he made an effort for words.

'I had been writing.'

'Writing what?'

Again the soldier looked him up and down. The officer could hear him panting. The smile came into the blue eyes. The soldier worked his dry throat, but could not speak. Suddenly the smile lit like a flame on the officer's face, and a kick came heavily against the orderly's thigh. The youth moved a pace sideways. His face went dead, with two black, staring eyes.

'Well?' said the officer.

The orderly's mouth had gone dry, and his tongue rubbed in it as on dry brown paper. He worked his throat. The officer raised his foot. The servant went stiff.

'Some poetry, Sir,' came the crackling, unrecognisable sound of his voice.

'Poetry, what poetry?' asked the captain, with a sickly smile.

Again there was the working in the throat. The captain's heart had suddenly gone down heavily, and he stood sick and tired.

'For my girl, Sir,' he heard the dry, inhuman sound.

'Oh!' he said, turning away. 'Clear the table.'

'Click!' – went the soldier's throat; then again, 'click!'; and then the half articulate:

'Yes Sir.'

The young soldier was gone, looking old, and walking heavily. The officer, left alone, held himself rigid, to prevent himself from thinking. His instinct warned him that he must not think. Deep inside him was the intense gratification of his passion, still working powerfully. Then there was a counteraction, a horrible breaking down of something inside him, a whole agony of reaction. He stood there for an hour motionless, a chaos of sensations, but rigid with a will to keep blank his consciousness, to prevent his mind grasping. And he held himself so until the worst of the stress had passed, when he began to drink, drank himself to an intoxication, till he slept obliterated. When he woke in the morning he was shaken to the base of his nature. But he had fought off the realisation of what he had done. He had prevented his mind from taking it in, had suppressed it along with his instincts, and the conscious man had nothing to do with it. He felt only as after a bout of intoxication, weak, but the affair itself all dim and not to be recovered. Of the drunkenness of his passion he successfully refused remembrance. And when his orderly appeared with coffee, the officer assumed the same self he had had the morning before. He refused the event of the past night – denied it had

ever been – and was successful in his denial. He
had not done any such thing – not he himself.
Whatever there might be lay at the door of a
stupid, insubordinate servant.

The orderly had gone about in a stupor all the
evening. He drank some beer because he was
parched, but not much, the alcohol made his
feeling come back, and he could not bear it. He
was dulled, as if nine-tenths of the ordinary man
in him were inert. He crawled about disfigured.
Still, when he thought of the kicks, he went sick,
and when he thought of the threats of more
kicking, in the room afterwards, his heart went
hot and faint, and he panted, remembering the
one that had come. He had been forced to say
'For my girl'. He was much too done even to
want to cry. His mouth hung slightly open, like
an idiot's. He felt vacant, and wasted. So, he
wandered at his work, painfully, and very slowly
and clumsily, fumbling blindly with the brushes,
and finding it difficult, when he sat down, to
summon the energy to move again. His limbs, his
jaw were slack and nerveless. But he was very
tired. He got to bed at last and slept inert, relaxed,
in a sleep that was rather stupor than slumber, a
dead night of stupefaction shot through with
gleams of anguish.

In the morning were the manoeuvres. But he
woke even before the bugle sounded. The painful
ache in his chest, the dryness of his throat, the
awful steady feeling of misery made his eyes come
awake and dreary at once. He knew without

thinking, what had happened. And he knew that
the day had come again, when he must go on
with his round. The last bit of darkness was being
pushed out of the room. He would have to move
his inert body and go on. He was so young, and
had known so little trouble, that he was bewildered. He only wished it would stay night, so that
he could lie still, covered up by the darkness. And
yet nothing would prevent the day from coming,
nothing would save him from having to get up,
and saddle the captain's horse, and make the
captain's coffee. It was there, inevitable. And
then, he thought, it was impossible. Yet they
would not leave him free. He must go and take
the coffee to the captain. He was too stunned to
understand it. He only knew it was inevitable –
inevitable, however long he lay inert.

At last, after heaving at himself, for he seemed
to be a mass of inertia, he got up. But he had to
force every one of his movements from behind,
with his will. He felt lost, and dazed, and helpless.
Then he clutched hold of the bed, the pain was so
keen. And looking at his thighs, he saw the darker
bruises on his swarthy flesh and he knew that, if he
pressed one of his fingers on one of the bruises, he
should faint. But he did not want to faint – he did
not want anybody to know. No one should ever
know. It was between him and the captain. There
were only the two people in the world now –
himself and the captain.

Slowly, economically, he got dressed and
forced himself to walk. Everything was obscure,

except just what he had his hands on. But he managed to get through his work. The very pain revived his dulled senses. The worst remained yet. He took the tray and went up to the captain's room. The officer, pale and heavy, sat at the table. The orderly, as he saluted, felt himself put out of existence. He stood still for a moment submitting to his own nullification – then he gathered himself, seemed to regain himself, and then the captain began to grow vague, unreal, and the younger soldier's heart beat up. He clung to this sensation – that the captain did not exist, so that he himself might live. But when he saw his officer's hand tremble as he took the coffee, he felt everything falling shattered. And he went away, feeling as if he himself were coming to pieces, disintegrated. And when the captain was there on horseback, giving orders, while he himself stood, with rifle and knapsack, sick with pain, he felt as if he must shut his eyes – as if he must shut his eyes on everything. It was only the long agony of marching with a parched throat that filled him with one single, sleep-heavy intention: to save himself.

He was getting used even to his parched throat. That the snowy peaks were radiant among the sky, that the whitey-green glacier river twisted through its pale shoals, in the valley below, seemed almost supernatural. But he was going mad with fever and thirst. He plodded on, uncomplaining. He did not want to speak, not to anybody. There were two gulls, like flakes of water and snow, over the river. The scent of green rye soaked in sunshine came like a sickness. And the march continued, monotonously, almost like a bad sleep.

At the next farmhouse, which stood low and broad near the highroad, tubs of water had been put out. The soldiers clustered round to drink. They took off their helmets, and the steam mounted from their wet hair. The captain sat on horseback, watching. He needed to see his orderly. His helmet threw a dark shadow over his light, fierce eyes, but his moustache and mouth and chin were distinct in the sunshine. The orderly must move under the presence of the figure of the horseman. It was not that he was afraid, or cowed. It was as if he were disembowelled, made empty, like an empty shell. He felt himself as nothing, a shadow creeping under the sunshine. And, thirsty as he was, he could scarcely drink, feeling the captain near him. He would not take off his helmet to wipe his wet hair. He wanted to stay in shadow, not to be forced into consciousness. Starting, he saw the light heel of the officer prick the belly of the horse; the captain cantered away, and he himself could relapse into vacancy.

Nothing, however, could give him back his living place in the hot, bright morning. He felt like a gap among it all. Whereas the captain was prouder, overriding. A hot flash went through the young servant's body. The captain was firmer and prouder with life, he himself was empty as a shadow. Again the flash went through him, dazing him out. But his heart ran a little firmer.

The company turned up the hill, to make a loop for the return. Below, from among the trees, the farm-bell clanged. He saw the labourers mowing barefoot at the thick grass leave off their work and go downhill, their scythes hanging over their shoulders, like long, bright claws curving down behind them. They seemed like dream-people, as if they had no relation to himself. He felt as in a blackish dream: as if all the other things were there and had form, but he himself was only a consciousness, a gap that could think and perceive.

The soldiers were tramping silently up the glaring hillside. Gradually his head began to revolve slowly, rhythmically. Sometimes it was dark before his eyes, as if he saw this world through a smoked glass, frail shadows and un-real. It gave him a pain in his head to walk.

The air was too scented, it gave no breath. All the lush green-stuff seemed to be issuing its sap, till the air was deathly, sickly with the smell of greenness. There was the perfume of clover, like pure honey and bees. Then there grew a faint acrid tang – they were near the beeches; and then a queer clattering noise, and a suffocating, hideous smell: they were passing a flock of sheep, a shepherd in a black smock, holding his hook. Why should the sheep huddle together under this fierce sun? He felt that the shepherd could not see him, though he could see the shepherd.

At last there was the halt. They stacked rifles in a conical stack, put down their kit in a scattered circle around it, and dispersed a little, sitting on a small knoll high on the hillside. The chatter began. The soldiers were steaming with heat, but were lively. He sat still, seeing the blue mountains rise upon the land, twenty kilometres away. There was a blue fold in the ranges, then out of that, at the foot, the broad pale bed of the river, stretches of whitey-green water between pinkish-grey shoals among the dark pine-woods. There it was, spread out a long way off. And it seemed to come downhill, the river. There was a raft being steered, a mile away. It was a strange country. Nearer, a red-roofed, broad farm with white base and square dots of windows crouched beside the wall of beech-foliage on the wood's edge. There were long strips of rye and clover and pale green corn. And just at his feet, below the knoll, was a darkish bog, where globe flowers stood breathless still on their slim stalks. And some of the pale gold bubbles were burst, and a broken fragment hung in the air. He thought he was going to sleep.

Suddenly something moved into this coloured mirage before his eyes. The captain, a small, light blue and scarlet figure, was trotting evenly between the strips of corn, along the level brow of the hill. And the man making flag-signals was coming on. – Proud and sure moved the horse-man figure, the quick, bright thing in which was concentrated all the light of this morning, which for the rest lay a fragile, shining shadow. Submissive, apathetic, the young soldier sat and stared. But as the horse slowed to a walk, coming up the last steep path, the great flash flared over the body and soul of the orderly. He sat waiting. The back of his head felt as if it were weighted with a heavy piece of fire. He did not want to eat. His hands trembled slightly as he moved them. Meanwhile the officer on horseback was approaching slowly and proudly. The tension grew in the orderly's soul. Then again, seeing the captain ease himself on the saddle, the flash blazed through him.

The captain looked at the patch of light blue and scarlet, and dark heads, scattered closely on the hillside. It pleased him. The command pleased him. And he was feeling proud. His orderly was among them in common subjection. The officer rose a little on his stirrups to look. The young soldier sat with averted, dumb face. The captain relaxed on his seat. His slim legged, beautiful horse, brown as a beech nut, walked proudly uphill. The captain passed into the zone of the company's atmosphere: a hot smell of men, of sweat, of leather. He knew it very well. After a word with the lieutenant, he went a few paces higher, and sat there, a dominant figure, his sweat-marked horse swishing its tail, while he looked down on his men, on his orderly, a nonentity among the crowd.

The young soldier's heart was like fire in his chest, and he breathed with difficulty. The officer, looking downhill, saw three of the young soldiers, two pails of water between them, staggering across a sunny green field. A table had been set up under a tree, and there the slim lieutenant stood importantly busy. Then the captain summoned himself to an act of courage. He called his orderly.

The flame leapt into the young soldier's throat as he heard the command, and he rose blindly, stifled. He saluted, standing below the officer. He did not look up. But there was the flicker in the captain's voice.

'Go to the inn and fetch me—' – the officer gave his commands. 'Quick!' he added.

At the last word, the heart of the servant leapt with a flash, and he felt the strength come over his body. But he turned in mechanical obedience, and set off at a heavy run downhill, looking almost like a bear, his trousers bagging over his military boots. And the officer watched this blind, plunging run all the way.

But it was only the outside of the orderly's body that was obeying so humbly and mechanically. Inside had gradually accumulated a core into which all the energy of that young life was compact and concentrated. He executed his commission, and plodded quickly back uphill. There was a pain in his head, as he walked, that made him twist his features unknowingly. But hard there in the centre of his chest was himself, himself, firm, and not to be plucked to pieces.

The captain had gone up into the wood. – The

orderly plodded through the hot, powerfully smelling zone of the company's atmosphere. He had a curious mass of energy inside him now. The captain was less real than himself. He approached the green entrance to the wood. There, in the half-shade, he saw the horse standing, the sunshine and the flickering shadow of leaves dancing over his brown body. There was a clearing where timber had lately been felled. Here, in the gold-green shade beside the brilliant cup of sunshine, stood two figures, blue and pink, the bits of pink showing out plainly. The captain was talking to his lieutenant.

The orderly stood on the edge of the bright clearing, where great trunks of trees, stripped and glistening, lay stretched like naked, brown-skinned bodies. Chips of wood littered the trampled floor, like splashed light, and the bases of the felled trees stood here and there, with their raw, level tops. Beyond was the brilliant, sunlit green of a beech.

'Then I will ride forward,' the orderly heard his captain say. The lieutenant saluted and strode away. He himself went forward. A hot flash passed through his belly, as he tramped towards his officer.

The captain watched the rather heavy figure of the young soldier stumble forward, and his veins ran too hot. This was to be man to man between them. He yielded before the solid, stumbling figure with bent head. The orderly stooped and put the food on a level-sawn tree-base. The captain watched the glistening, sun-inflamed,

naked hands. He wanted to speak to the young
soldier, but could not. The servant propped a
bottle against his thigh, pressed open the cork, and
poured out the beer into the mug. He kept his
head bent. The captain accepted the mug.

'Hot!' he said, as if amiably.

The flame sprang out of the orderly's heart,
nearly suffocating him.

'Yes Sir,' he replied, between shut teeth.

And he heard the sound of the captain's
drinking, and he clenched his fists, such a strong
torment came into his wrists. Then came the faint
clang of the closing of the pot-lid. He looked up.
The captain was watching him. He glanced
swiftly away. Then he saw the officer stoop and
take a piece of bread from the tree-base. Again the
flash of flame went through the young soldier,
seeing the stiff body stoop beneath him, and his
hands jerked. He looked away. He could feel the
officer was nervous. The bread fell as it was being
broken. The officer ate the other piece. The two
men stood tense and still, the master laboriously
chewing his bread, the servant staring with
averted face, his fists clenched.

Then the young soldier started. The officer had
pressed open the lid of the mug again. The orderly
watched the lid of the mug, and the white hand
that clenched the handle, as if he were fascinated.
It was raised. The youth followed it with his eyes.
And then he saw the thin, strong throat of the
elder man moving up and down as he drank, the
strong jaw working. And the instinct which had

been jerking at the young man's wrists suddenly jerked free. He jumped, feeling as if he were rent in two by a strong flame.

The spur of the officer caught in a tree-root, he went down backwards with a crash, the middle of his back thudding sickeningly against the sharp-edged tree-base, the pot flying away. And in a second the orderly, with serious, earnest young face, and underlip between his teeth, had got his knee in the officer's chest and was pressing the chin backward over the farther edge of the tree-stump, pressing, with all his heart behind in a passion of relief, the tension of his wrists exquisite with relief. And with the base of his palms he shoved at the chin, with all his might. And it was pleasant too to have that chin, that hard jaw already slightly rough with beard, in his hands. He did not relax one hair's-breadth but, all the force of all his blood exulting in his thrust, he shoved back the head of the other man, till there was a little 'cluck' and a crunching sensation. Then he felt as if his heart went to vapour. Heavy convulsions shook the body of the offi-cer, frightening and horrifying the young soldier. Yet it pleased him too to repress them. It pleased him to keep his hands pressing back the chin, to feel the chest of the other man yield in expiration to the weight of his strong young knee, to feel the hard twitchings of the prostrate body jerking his own whole frame, which was pressed down on it.

But it went still. He could look into the nostrils of the other man, the eyes he could scarcely see.

How curiously the mouth was pushed out, exaggerating the full lips, and the moustache bristling up from them. Then, with a start, he noticed the nostrils gradually filled with blood. The red brimmed, hesitated, ran over, and went in a thin trickle down the face to the eyes.

It shocked and distressed him. Slowly, he got up. The body twitched and sprawled there inert. He stood and looked at it in silence. It was a pity *it* was broken. It represented more than the thing which had kicked and bullied him. He was afraid to look at the eyes. They were hideous now, only the whites showing, and the blood running to them. The face of the orderly was drawn with horror at the sight. Well, it was so. In his heart he was satisfied. He had hated the face of the captain. It was extinguished now. There was a heavy relief in the orderly's soul. That was as it should be. But he could not bear to see the long, military body lying broken over the tree-base, the fine fingers crisped. He wanted to hide it away.

Quickly, busily, he gathered it up and pushed it under the felled tree-trunks, which rested their beautiful smooth length either end on logs. The face was horrible with blood. He covered it with the helmet. Then he pushed the limbs straight and decent, and brushed the dead leaves off the fine cloth of the uniform. So, it lay quite still in the shadow under there. A little strip of sunshine ran along the breast, from a chink between the logs. The orderly sat by it for a few moments. Here his own life also ended.

Then, through his daze, he heard the lieutenant, in a loud voice, explaining to the men outside the wood that they were to suppose the bridge on the river was held by the enemy. Now they were to march to the attack in such and such a manner. The lieutenant had no gift of expression. The orderly, listening from habit, got muddled. And when the lieutenant began it all again, he ceased to hear.

He knew he must go. He stood up. It surprised him that the leaves were glittering in the sun, and the chips of wood reflecting white from the ground. For him a change had come over the world. But for the rest it had not – all seemed the same. Only he had left it. And he could not go back. – It was his duty to return with the beer-pot and the bottle. He could not. He had left all that. The lieutenant was still hoarsely explaining. He must go, or they would overtake him. And he could not bear contact with anyone now.

He drew his fingers over his eyes, trying to find out where he was. Then he turned away. He saw the horse standing in the path. He went up to it and mounted. It hurt him to sit in the saddle. The pain of keeping his seat occupied him as they cantered through the wood. He would not have minded anything, but he could not get away from the sense of being divided from the others. The path led out of the trees. On the edge of the wood he pulled up and stood watching. There in the spacious sunshine of the valley soldiers were

moving in a little swarm. Every now and then, a
man harrowing on a strip of fallow shouted to his
oxen, at the turn. The village and the white-
towered church was small in the sunshine. And he
no longer belonged to it – he sat there, beyond,
like a man outside in the dark. He had gone out
from everyday life into the unknown, and he
could not, he even did not want to go back.

Turning from the sun-blazing valley, he rode
deep into the wood. Tree-trunks, like people
standing grey and still, took no notice as he
went. A doe, herself a moving bit of sunshine
and shadow, went running through the flecked
shade. There were bright green rents in the
foliage. Then it was all pine-wood, dark and
cool. And he was sick with pain, he had an
intolerable great pulse in his head, and he was
sick. He had never been ill in his life. He felt lost,
quite dazed with all this.

Trying to get down from the horse, he fell,
astonished at the pain and his lack of balance. The
horse shifted uneasily. He jerked its bridle and set
it cantering jerkily away. It was his last connection
with the rest of things.

But he only wanted to lie down and not be
disturbed. Stumbling through the trees, he came
on a quiet place where beeches and pine trees
grew on a slope. Immediately he had laid down
and closed his eyes, his consciousness went racing
on without him. A big pulse of sickness beat in
him as if it throbbed through the whole earth. He
was burning with dry heat. But he was too busy,

too tearingly active in the incoherent race of delirium, to observe.

He came to with a start. His mouth was dry and hard, his heart beat heavily, but he had not the energy to get up. His heart beat heavily. Where was he? – the barracks, – at home? There was something knocking. And, making an effort, he looked round – trees, and glitter of greenery, and reddish bright, still pieces of sunshine on the floor. He did not believe he was himself, he did not believe what he saw. Something was knocking. He made a struggle towards consciousness, but relapsed. Then he struggled again. And gradually his surroundings fell into relationship with himself. He knew, and a great pang of fear went through his heart. Somebody was knocking. He could see the heavy, black rags of a fir-tree overhead. Then everything went black. Yet he did not believe he had closed his eyes. He had not. Out of the blackness sight slowly emerged again. And someone was knocking. Quickly, he saw the blood-disfigured face of his captain, which he hated. And he held himself still with horror. Yet, deep inside him, he knew that it was so, the captain should be dead. But the physical delirium got hold of him. Someone was knocking. He lay perfectly still, as if dead, with fear. And he went unconscious.

When he opened his eyes again, he started, seeing something creeping swiftly up a tree-trunk. It was a little bird. And a bird was whistling overhead. Tap-tap-tap — it was the small, quick bird rapping the tree-trunk with its beak, as if its head were a little round hammer. He watched it curiously. It shifted sharply, in its creeping fashion. Then, like a mouse, it slid down the bare trunk. Its swift creeping sent a flash of revulsion through him. He raised his head. It felt a great weight. Then, the little bird ran out of the shadows across a still patch of sunshine, its little head bobbing swiftly, its white legs twinkling brightly for a moment. How neat it was in its build, so compact, with pieces of white on its wings. There were several of them. They were so pretty — but they crept like swift, erratic mice, running here and there among the beech-mast.

He lay down again exhausted, and his consciousness lapsed. He had a horror of the little creeping birds. All his blood seemed to be darting and creeping in his head. And yet he could not move.

He came to with a further ache of exhaustion. There was the pain in his head, and the horrible sickness, and his inability to move. He had never been ill in his life. He did not know where he was or what he was. Probably he had got sunstroke. Or what else? — he had silenced the captain for ever — some time ago — oh, a long time ago. There had been blood on his face, and his eyes had turned upwards. It was all right, somehow. It was peace. But now he had got beyond himself. He had never been here before. Was it life, or not-life? He was by himself. They were in a big, bright place, those others, and he was outside. The town, all the country, a big bright place of light: and he was outside, here, in the darkened open beyond, where each thing existed alone. But they would all have to come out there sometime, those others. Little, and left behind him, they all were. There had been father and mother and sweetheart. What did they all matter. This was the open land.

He sat up. Something scuffled. It was a little brown squirrel running in lovely, undulating bounds over the floor, its red tail completing the undulation of its body – and then, as it sat up, furling and unfurling. He watched it, pleased. It ran on again, friskily, enjoying itself. It flew wildly at another squirrel, and they were chasing each other, and making little scolding, chattering noises. The soldier wanted to speak to them. But only a hoarse sound came out of his throat. The squirrels burst away – they flew up the trees. And then he saw the one peeping round at him, half way up a tree-trunk. A start of fear went through him, though, in so far as he was conscious, he was amused. It still stayed, its little keen face staring at him half way up the tree-trunk, its little ears pricked up, its clawey little hands clinging to the bark, its white breast reared. He started from it in panic.

Struggling to his feet, he lurched away. He went on walking, walking, looking for something – for a drink. His brain felt hot and inflamed for want of water. He stumbled on.

Then he did not know anything. He went unconscious as he walked. Yet he stumbled on, his mouth open.

When, to his dumb wonder, he opened his eyes on the world again, he no longer tried to remember what it was. There was thick, golden light behind golden-tree glitterings, and tall, grey-purple shafts, and darknesses further off, surrounding him, growing deeper. He was conscious of a sense of arrival. He was amid the reality, on the real, dark bottom. But there was the thirst burning in his brain. He felt lighter, not so heavy. He supposed it was newness. The air was muttering with thunder. He thought he was walking wonderfully swiftly and was coming straight to relief – or was it to water?

Suddenly he stood still with fear. There was a tremendous flare of gold, immense – just a few dark trunks like bars between him and it. All the young level wheat was burnished, gold glaring on its silky green. A woman, full-skirted, a black cloth on her head for head dress, was passing like a block of shadow through the glistering green corn, into the full glare. There was a farm, too, pale blue in shadow, and the timber black. And there was a church spire nearly fused away in the gold. The woman moved on, away from him. He had no language with which to speak to her. She was the bright, solid unreality. She would make a noise of words that would confuse him, and her eyes would look at him without seeing him. She

was crossing there to the other side. He stood
against a tree.

When at last he turned, looking down the long,
bare groove whose flat bed was already filling dark,
he saw the mountains in a wonder-light, not far
away, and radiant. Behind the soft, grey ridge of
the nearest range the further mountains stood
golden and pale grey, the snow all radiant like
pure, soft gold. So still, gleaming in the sky,
fashioned pure out of the ore of the sky, they
shone in their silence. He stood and looked at
them, his face illuminated. And like the golden,
lustrous gleaming of the snow he felt his own thirst
bright in him. He stood and gazed, leaning against
a tree. And then everything slid away into space.

During the night the lightning fluttered perpe-
tually, making the whole sky white. He must have
walked again. The world hung livid around him
for moments, fields a level sheen of grey-green
light, trees in dark bulk, and a range of clouds
black across a white sky. Then the darkness fell
like a shutter, and the night was whole. A faint
flutter of a half-revealed world, that could not
quite leap out of the darkness! – Then there again
stood a sweep of pallor for the land, dark shapes
looming, a range of clouds hanging overhead.
The world was a ghostly shadow, thrown for a
moment upon the pure darkness, which returned
ever whole and complete.

And the mere delirium of sickness and fever
went on inside him – his brain opening and
shutting like the night – then sometimes convul-

sions of terror from something with great eyes that stared round a tree – then the long agony of the march, and the sun decomposing his blood – then the pang of hate for the captain, followed by a pang of tenderness and ease. But everything was distorted, born of an ache and resolving into an ache.

In the morning he came definitely awake. Then his brain flamed with the sole horror of thirstiness. The sun was on his face, the dew was steaming from his wet clothes. Like one possessed, he got up. There, straight in front of him, blue and cool and tender, the mountains ranged across the pale edge of the morning sky. He wanted them – he wanted them alone – he wanted to leave himself and be identified with them. They did not move, they were still and soft, with white, gentle markings of snow. He stood still, mad with suffering, his hands crisping and clutching. Then he was twisting in a paroxysm on the grass.

He lay still, in a kind of dream of anguish. His thirst seemed to have separated itself from him, and to stand apart, a single demand. Then the pain he felt was another single self. Then there was the clog of his body, another separate thing. He was divided among all kinds of separate beings. There was some strange, agonised connection between them, but they were drawing further apart. Then they would all split. The sun, drilling down on him, was drilling through the bond. Then they would all fall, fall through the everlasting lapse of space.

Then again his consciousness reasserted itself. He roused onto his elbow and stared at the gleaming mountains. There they ranked, all still and wonderful between earth and heaven. He stared till his eyes went black, and the mountains as they stood in their beauty, so clean and cool, seemed to have it, that which was lost in him.

When the soldiers found him, three hours later, he was lying with his face over his arm, his black hair giving off heat under the sun. But he was still alive. Seeing the open, black mouth the young soldiers dropped him in horror.

He died in the hospital at night, without having seen again.

The doctors saw the bruises on his legs, behind, and were silent.

The bodies of the two men lay together, side by side, in the mortuary, the one white and slender, but laid rigidly at rest, the other looking as if every moment it must rouse into life again, so young and unused, from a slumber.

Second-Best

'Oh, I'm tired!' Frances exclaimed petulantly, and in the same instant she dropped down on the turf near the hedge-bottom. Anne stood a moment surprised, then, accustomed to the vagaries of her beloved Frances, said:

'Well, and aren't you always likely to be tired, after travelling that blessed long way from Liverpool yesterday!' and she plumped down beside her sister. Anne was a wise young body of fourteen, very buxom, brimming with common-sense. Frances was much older, about twenty-three, and whimsical, spasmodic. She was the beauty and the clever child of the family. She plucked the goose-grass buttons from her dress in a nervous, desperate fashion. Her beautiful profile, looped above with black hair, warm with the dusky-and-scarlet complexion of a pear, was calm as a mask, her thin brown hand plucked nervously.

'It's not the journey,' she said, objecting to Anne's obtuseness. Anne looked inquiringly at her darling. The young girl, in her self-confident,

practical way, proceeded to reckon up this
whimsical creature. But suddenly she found
herself full in the eyes of Frances; felt two dark,
hectic eyes flaring challenge at her, and she shrank
away. Frances was peculiar for these great, exposed looks, which disconcerted people by their
violence and their suddenness.

'What's the matter, poor old duck?' asked
Anne, as she folded the slight, wilful form of her
sister in her arms. Frances laughed shakily, and
nestled down for comfort on the budding breasts
of the strong girl.

'Oh, I'm only a bit tired,' she murmured, on
the point of tears.

'Well of course you are, what do you expect?'
soothed Anne. It was a joke to Frances that Anne
should play elder, almost mother to her. But then,
Anne was in her unvexed teens; men were like
big dogs to her: while Frances, at twenty-three,
suffered a good deal.

The country was intensely morning-still. On
the common everything shone beside its shadow,
and the hillside gave off heat in silence. The
brown turf seemed in a low state of combustion,
the leaves of the oaks were scorched brown.
Among the blackish foliage in the distance shone
the small red and orange of the village.

The willows in the brook-course at the foot of
the common suddenly shook with a dazzling
effect like diamonds. It was a puff of wind. Anne
resumed her normal position. She spread her
knees, and put in her lap a handful of hazel

nuts, whitey-green leafy things, whose one cheek was tanned between brown and pink. These she began to crack and eat. Frances, with bowed head, mused bitterly.

'Eh, you know Tom Smedley?' began the young girl, as she pulled a tight kernel out of its shell.

'I suppose so,' replied Frances sarcastically.

'Well, he gave me a wild rabbit what he'd caught, to keep with my tame ones – and it's living.'

'That's a good thing,' said Frances, very detached and ironic.

'Well, it *is*! He reckoned he'd take me to Ollerton Feast, but he never did. Look here, he took a servant from the rectory, I saw him.'

'So he ought,' said Frances.

'No he oughtn't! And I told him so – and I told him I should tell you – an' I have done.'

Click and snap went a nut between her teeth. She sorted out the kernel, and chewed complacently.

'It doesn't make much difference,' said Frances.

'Well – 'appen it doesn't – but I was mad with him all the same.'

'Why?'

'Because I was: he's no right to go with a servant.'

'He's a perfect right,' persisted Frances, very just and cold.

'No he hasn't, when he'd said he'd take me.'

Frances burst into a laugh of amusement and relief.

'Oh no, I'd forgot that,' she said – adding: 'And what did he say when you promised to tell me?'

'He laughed, and said "She won't fret her fat over that."'

'And she won't,' sniffed Frances.

There was silence. The common, with its sere, blonde headed thistles, its heaps of silent bramble, its brown-husked gorse, in the glare of sunshine seemed visionary. Across the brook began the immense pattern of agriculture, white chequering of barley stubble, brown squares of wheat, khaki patches of pasture, red stripes of fallow, with the woodland and the tiny village dark like ornaments, leading away to the distance, right to the hills, where the check-pattern grew smaller and smaller, till in the blackish haze of heat, far-off, only the tiny white squares of barley stubble showed distinct.

'Eh, I say, here's a rabbit-hole!' cried Anne suddenly.

'Should we watch if one comes out? You won't have to fidget, you know.'

The two girls sat perfectly still. Frances watched certain objects in her surroundings: they had a peculiar, unfriendly look about them: the weight of greenish elderberries on their purpling stalks; the twinkling of the yellowing crab-apples that clustered high up in the hedge, against the sky; the exhausted, limp leaves of the primroses lying flat in the hedge-bottom: all looked strange to her. Then her eyes caught a movement. A mole was moving silently over the warm, red soil, nosing, shuffling hither and thither, flat and dark as a shadow, shifting about, and as suddenly brisk, and as silent, like a very ghost of joie de vivre. Frances started, from habit was about to call on Anne to kill the little pest. But today her lethargy of unhappiness was too much for her. She watched the little brute paddling, snuffing, touching things to discover them, running in blindness, delighted to ecstasy by the sunlight and the hot strange things that caressed its belly and its nose.

She felt a keen pity for the little creature.

'Eh, our Fran, look there! It's a mole.'

Anne was on her feet, standing watching the dark, unconscious beast. Frances frowned with anxiety.

'It doesn't run off, does it?' said the young girl softly. Then she steathily approached the creature. The mole paddled fumblingly away. In an instant Anne put her foot upon it, not too heavily. Frances could see the struggling, swimming movement of the little pink hands of the brute, the twisting and twitching of its pointed nose, as it wrestled under the sole of the boot.

'It *does* wriggle!' said the bonny girl, knitting her brows in a frown at the eerie sensation. Then she bent down to look at her trap. Frances could now see, beyond the edge of the boot-sole, the heaving of the velvet shoulders, the pitiful turning of the sightless face, the frantic rowing of the flat, pink hands.

'Kill the thing,' she said, turning away her face.

'Oo – I'm not,' laughed Anne, shrinking. 'You can if you like.'

'I *don't* like,' said Frances, with quiet intensity.

After several dabbling attempts, Anne succeeded in picking up the little animal by the scruff of its neck. It threw back its head, flung its long blind snout from side to side, the mouth open in a peculiar oblong, with tiny pinkish teeth at the edge. The blind, frantic mouth gaped and writhed. The body, heavy and clumsy, hung scarcely moving.

'Isn't it a snappy little thing,' observed Anne, twisting to avoid the teeth.

'What are you going to do with it?' asked Frances sharply.

'It's got to be killed – look at the damage they do. I s'll take it home and let Dadda or somebody kill it. I'm not going to let it go.'

She swaddled the creature clumsily in her pocket-handkerchief, and sat down beside her sister. There was an interval of silence, during which Anne combated the efforts of the mole.

'You've not had much to say about Jimmy this time. Did you see him often in Liverpool?' Anne asked suddenly.

'Once or twice,' replied Frances, giving no sign of how the question troubled her.

'And aren't you sweet on him any more, then?'

'I should think I'm not, seeing that he's engaged.'

'Engaged! Jimmy Barrass! Well of all things! I never thought *he'd* get engaged.'

'Why not, he's as much right as anybody else?' snapped Frances. Anne was fumbling with the mole.

''Appen so,' she said at length. 'But I never thought Jimmy would, though.'

'Why not?' snapped Frances.

'*I* don't know. – This blessed mole, it'll not keep still! – Who's he got engaged to?'

'How should I know.'

'I thought you'd ask him, you've known him long enough. – I s'd think he thought he'd get engaged now he's a Doctor of Chemistry.'

Frances laughed in spite of herself.

'What's that got to do with it,' she asked.

'I'm sure it's got a lot. He'll want to feel *somebody* now, so he's got engaged. – Hey, stop it, go in!'

But at this juncture the mole almost succeeded in wriggling clear. It wrestled and twisted frantically, waved its pointed blind head, its mouth standing open like a little shaft, its big wrinkled hands spread out.

'Go in with you!' urged Anne, poking the little creature with her forefinger, trying to get it back into the handkerchief. Suddenly the mouth turned like a spark on her finger.

'Oh!' she cried. 'He's bit me.'

She dropped him to the floor. Dazed, the blind

creature fumbled round. Frances felt like shriek-
ing: she expected him to dart away in a flash, like a
mouse, and there he remained groping; she
wanted to cry to him to be gone. Anne, in a
sudden decision of wrath, caught up her sister's
walking-cane. With one blow, the mole was
dead. Frances was startled and shocked. One
moment, the little wretch was fussing in the
heat, and the next it lay like a little bag, inert
and black: not a struggle, scarce a quiver.

'It is dead!' Frances said breathlessly.

Anne took her finger from her mouth, looked
at the tiny pinpricks, and said:

'Yes he is, and I'm glad. They're vicious little
nuisances, moles are.'

With which her wrath vanished. She picked up
the dead animal.

'Hasn't it got a beautiful skin,' she mused,
stroking the fur with her forefinger, then with
her cheek.

'Mind,' said Frances sharply. 'You'll have the
blood on your skirt!'

One ruby drop of blood hung on the small
snout, ready to fall. Anne shook it off onto some
harebells. Frances suddenly became calm; in that
moment, grown-up.

'I suppose they *have* to be killed,' she said, and a
certain rather dreary indifference succeeded to her
grief. The twinkling crab-apples, the glitter of
brilliant willows now seemed to her trifling,
scarcely worth the notice. Something had died
in her, so that things lost their poignancy. She was

calm, indifference overlying her quiet sadness. Rising, she walked down to the brook course.

'Here, wait for me,' cried Anne, coming tumbling after. Frances stood on the bridge, looking at the red mud trodden into pockets by the feet of cattle. There was not a drain of water left, but everything smelled green, succulent. Why did she care so little for Anne, who was so fond of her, she asked herself. Why did she care so little for anyone. She did not know, but she felt a rather stubborn pride in her isolation and indifference.

They entered a field where stooks of barley stood in rows, the straight, blonde tresses of the corn streaming onto the ground. The stubble was bleached by the intense summer, so that the expanse glared white. The next field was sweet and soft with a second crop of seeds, thin, straggling clover whose little pink knobs rested prettily in the dark green. The scent was faint and sickly. The girls came up in single file, Frances leading.

Near the gate, a young man was mowing with the scythe some fodder for the afternoon feed of the cattle. As he saw the girls, he left off working and waited in an aimless kind of way. Frances was dressed in white muslin, and she walked with dignity, detached and forgetful. Her lack of agitation, her simple, unheeding advance made him nervous. She had loved the far-off Jimmy for five years, having had in return his half-measures. This man only affected her slightly.

Tom was of medium stature, energetic in build. His smooth, fair skinned face was burned red, not brown, by the sun, and this ruddiness enhanced his appearance of good humour and easiness. Being a year older than Frances, he would have courted her long ago had she been so inclined. As it was, he had gone his uneventful way amiably, chatting with many a girl, but remaining unattached, free of trouble for the most part. Only he knew he wanted a woman. He hitched his trousers just a trifle self-consciously as the girls approached. Frances was a rare, delicate kind of being, whom he realised with a queer and delicious stimulation in his veins. She gave him a slight sense of suffocation: somehow, this morning, she affected him more than usual. She was dressed in white. He, however, being matter-of-fact in his mind, did not realise. His feeling had never become conscious, purposive.

Frances knew what she was about. Tom was ready to love her as soon as she would show him. Now that she could not have Jimmy, she did not poignantly care. Still, she would have something. If she could not have the best – Jimmy, whom she knew to be something of a snob – she would have the second best, Tom. She advanced rather indifferently.

'You are back then!' said Tom. She marked the touch of uncertainty in his voice.

'No,' she laughed. 'I'm still in Liverpool,' and the undertone of intimacy made him burn.

'This isn't you, then?' he asked.

Her heart leapt up in approval. She looked in his eyes, and for a second, was with him.

'Why, what do you think?' she laughed.

He lifted his hat from his head with a distracted little gesture. – She liked him, his quaint ways, his humour, his ignorance, and his slow masculinity.

'Here, look here Tom Smedley,' broke in Anne.

'A moudiwarp! – Did you find it dead?' he asked.

'No, it bit me,' said Anne.

'Oh ay! – an' that got your rag out, did it?'

'No, it didn't!' Anne scolded sharply. 'Such language!'

'Oh – what's up wi' it?'

'I can't bear you to talk broad.'

'Can't you?'

He glanced at Frances.

'It isn't nice,' Frances said. She did not care, really. The vulgar speech jarred on her as a rule; Jimmy was a gentleman. But Tom's manner of speech did not matter to her.

'I like you to talk *nicely*,' she added.

'Do you?' he replied, tilting his hat, stirred.

'And generally you *do*, you know,' she smiled.

'I s'll have to have a try,' he said, rather tensely gallant.

'What?' she asked brightly.

'To talk nice to you,' he said. Frances coloured furiously, bent her head for a moment, then laughed gaily, as if she liked this clumsy hint.

'Eh now, you mind what you're saying,' cried Anne, giving the young man an admonitory pat.

'You wouldn't have to give yon mole many knocks like *that*,' he teased, relieved to get on safe ground, rubbing his arm.

'No indeed, it died in one blow,' said Frances, with a flippancy that was hateful to her.

'You're not so good at knockin' 'em?' he said, turning to her.

'I don't know, if I'm cross,' she said, decisively.

'No?' he replied, with alert attentiveness.

'I could,' she added, harder, 'if it was necessary.'

He was slow to feel her difference.

'And don't you consider it *is* necessary?' he asked, with misgiving.

'We – ell – is it?' she said, looking at him steadily, coldly.

'I reckon it is,' he replied, looking away, but standing stubborn.

She laughed quickly.

'But it isn't necessary for *me*,' she said, with slight contempt.

'Yes, that's quite true,' he answered.

She laughed in a shaky fashion.

'*I know it is*,' she said; and there was an awkward pause.

'Why, would you *like* me to kill moles then?' she asked, tentatively, after a while.

'They do do us a lot of damage,' he said, standing firm on his ground, angered.

'Well, I'll see, the next time I come across one,' she promised, defiantly. Their eyes met, and she sank before him, her pride troubled. He felt uneasy and triumphant and baffled, as if fate had gripped him. She smiled as she departed.

'Well,' said Anne, as the sisters went through the wheat stubble. 'I don't know what you two's been jawing about, I'm sure.'

'Don't you,' laughed Frances, significantly.

'No I don't. But at any rate, Tom Smedley's a good deal better to my thinking than Jimmy, so there – and nicer.'

'Perhaps he is,' said Frances coldly.

And the next day, after a secret, persistent hunt, she found another mole playing in the heat. She killed it, and in the evening, when Tom came to the gate to smoke his pipe after supper, she took him the dead creature.

'Here you are then!' she said.

'Did you catch it?' he replied, taking the velvet corpse into his fingers and examining it minutely. This was to hide his trepidation.

'Did you think I couldn't?' she asked, her face very near his.

'Nay, I didn't know.'

She laughed in his face, a strange little laugh that caught her breath, all agitation and tears and recklessness of desire. He looked frightened and upset. She put her hand on his arm.

'Shall you go out wi' me?' he asked, in a difficult, troubled tone.

She turned her face away, with a shaky laugh. The blood came up in him, strong, overmastering. He resisted it. But it drove him down, and he was carried away. Seeing the winsome, frail nape of her neck, fierce love came upon him for her, and tenderness.

'We s'll 'ave to tell your mother,' he said. And he stood, suffering, resisting his passion for her.

'Yes,' she replied, in a dead voice. But there was a thrill of pleasure in this death.

Jimmy and the Desperate Woman

'He is very fine and strong somewhere, but he does need a level-headed woman to look after him.'

That was the *friendly* feminine verdict upon him. It flattered him, it pleased him, it galled him.

Having divorced a very charming and clever wife, who had held this opinion for ten years, and at last had got tired of the level-headed protective game, his gall was uppermost.

'I want to throw Jimmy out on the world, but I know the poor little man will go and fall on some woman's bosom. That's the worst of him. If he could only stand alone for ten minutes. But he can't. At the same time, there *is* something fine about him, something rare.'

This had been Clarissa's summing-up as she floated away in the arms of the rich young American. The rich young American got rather angry when Jimmy's name was mentioned. Clarissa was now *his* wife. But she did sometimes talk as if she were still married to Jimmy.

Not in Jimmy's estimation, however. That worm had turned. Gall was uppermost. Gall and wormwood. He knew exactly what Clarissa thought – and said – about him. And the 'something fine, something rare, something strong' which he was supposed to have 'about him' was utterly outbalanced, in his feelings at least, by the 'poor little man' nestled upon 'some woman's bosom', which he was supposed to *be*.

'I am *not*,' he said to himself, 'a poor little man nestled upon some woman's bosom. If I could only find the right sort of woman, she should nestle on mine.'

Jimmy was now thirty-five, and this point, to nestle or to be nestled, was the emotional crux and turning-point.

He imagined to himself some really *womanly* woman, to whom he should be *only* 'fine and strong', and not for one moment 'the poor little man'. Why not some simple uneducated girl, some Tess of the D'Urbervilles, some wistful Gretchen, some humble Ruth gleaning an aftermath? Why not? Surely the world was full of such!

The trouble was he never met them. He only met sophisticated women. He really never had a chance of meeting 'real' people. So few of us ever do. Only the people we *don't* meet are the 'real' people, the simple, genuine, direct, spontaneous, unspoilt souls. Ah, the simple, genuine, unspoilt people we *don't* meet! What a tragedy it is!

Because, of course, they must be there! Somewhere! Only we never come across them.

Jimmy was terribly handicapped by his position. It brought him into contact with so many people. Only never the right sort. Never the 'real' people: the simple, genuine, unspoilt, etc., etc.

He was editor of a high-class, rather highbrow, rather successful magazine, and his rather personal, very candid editorials brought him shoals, swarms, hosts of admiring acquaintances. Realize that he was handsome, and could be extraordinarily 'nice', when he liked, and was really very clever, in his own critical way, and you see how many chances he had of being adored and protected.

In the first place his good looks: the fine, clean lines of his face, like the face of the laughing faun in one of the faun's unlaughingly, moody moments. The long, clean lines of the cheeks, the strong chin and the slightly arched, full nose, the beautiful dark-grey eyes with long lashes, and the thick black brows. In his mocking moments, when he seemed most himself, it was a pure Pan face, with thick black eyebrows cocked up, and grey eyes with a sardonic goaty gleam, and nose and mouth curling with satire. A good-looking, smooth-skinned satyr. That was Jimmy at his best. In the opinion of his men friends.

In his own opinion, he was a sort of Martyred Saint Sebastian, at whom the wicked world shot arrow after arrow – Mater Dolorosa nothing to him – and he counted the drops of blood as they fell: when he could keep count. Sometimes – as for instance when Clarissa said she was really departing with a rich young American, and should she divorce Jimmy, or was Jimmy going to divorce her? – then the arrows assailed him like a flight of starlings flying straight at him, jabbing at him, and the drops of martyred blood simply spattered down, he couldn't keep count.

So, naturally, he divorced Clarissa.

In the opinion of his men friends, he was, or should be, a consistently grinning faun, satyr, or Pan-person. In his own opinion, he was a Martyred Saint Sebastian with the mind of a Plato. In the opinion of his woman friends, he was a fascinating little man with a profound understanding of life and the capacity really to understand a woman and to make a woman feel a queen; which of course was to make a woman feel her *real* self . . .

He might, naturally, have made rich and resounding marriages, especially after the divorce. He didn't. The reason was, secretly, his resolve never to make any woman feel a queen any more. It was the turn of the women to make him feel a king.

Some unspoilt, unsophisticated, wild-blooded woman, to whom he would be a sort of Solomon of wisdom, beauty, and wealth. She would need to be in reduced circumstances to appreciate his wealth, which amounted to the noble sum of three thousand pounds and a little weekending cottage in Hampshire. And to be unsophisticated she would have to be a woman of the people. Absolutely.

At the same time, not just the 'obscure vulgar simplican'.

He received many letters, many, many, many, enclosing poems, stories, articles, or more personal unbosomings. He read them all: like a solemn rook pecking and scratching among the litter.

And one – not one letter, but one correspondent – might be *the* one – Mrs Emilia Pinnegar, who wrote from a mining village in Yorkshire. She was, of course, unhappily married.

Now Jimmy had always had a mysterious feeling about these dark and rather dreadful mining villages in the north. He himself had scarcely set foot north of Oxford. He felt that these miners up there must be the real stuff. And Pinnegar was a name, surely! And Emilia!

She wrote a poem, with a brief little note, that, if the editor of the *Commentator* thought the verses of no value, would he simply destroy them. Jimmy, as editor of the *Commentator*, thought the verses quite good and admired the brevity of the note. But he wasn't sure about printing the poem. He wrote back, Had Mrs Pinnegar nothing else to submit?

Then followed a correspondence. And at length, upon request, this from Mrs Pinnegar:

'You ask me about myself, but what shall I say? I am a woman of thirty-one, with one child, a girl of eight, and I am married to a man who lives in the same house with me, but goes to another woman. I try to write poetry, if it is poetry, because I have no other way of expressing myself at all, and even if it doesn't matter to anybody besides myself, I feel I must and will express myself, if only to save myself from developing cancer or some disease that women have. I was a schoolteacher before I was married, and I got my certificates at Rotherham College. If I could, I would teach again, and live alone. But married women teachers can't get jobs any more, they aren't allowed—'

THE COALMINER
BY HIS WIFE

THE donkey-engine's beating noise.
And the rattle, rattle of the sorting screens
Come down on me like the beat of his heart,
And mean the same as his breathing means.

The burning big pit-hill with fumes
Fills the air like the presence of that fair-haired
 man.
And the burning fire burning deeper and
 deeper
Is his will insisting since time began.

As he breathes the chair goes up and down
In the pit-shaft; he lusts as the wheel-fans spin
The sucking air: he lives in the coal
Underground: and his soul is a strange engine.

That is the matter of man he is.
I married him and I should know.
The mother earth from bowels of coal
Brought him forth for the overhead woe.

This was the poem that the editor of the *Commentator* hesitated about. He reflected, also, that Mrs Pinnegar didn't sound like one of the nestling, unsophisticated rustic type. It was something else that still attracted him: something desperate in a woman, something tragic.

THE NEXT EVENT

IF at evening, when the twilight comes,
　　You ask me what the day has been,
I shall not know. The distant drums
　　Of some newcomer intervene

Between me and the day that's been.
　　Some strange man leading long columns
Of unseen soldiers through the green
　　Sad twilight of these smoky slums.

And as the darkness slowly numbs
　　My senses, everything I've seen
Or heard the daylight through, becomes
　　Rubbish behind an opaque screen.

Instead, the sound of muffled drums
　　Inside myself: I have to lean
And listen as my strength succumbs,
　　To hear what these oncomings mean.

Perhaps the Death-God striking his thumbs
　　On the drums in a deadly rat-ta-ta-plan.
Or a strange man marching slow as he strums
　　The tune of a new weird hope in Man.

What does it matter! The day that began
   In coal-dust is ending the same, in crumbs
Of darkness like coal. I live if I can;
   If I can't, then I welcome whatever comes.

This poem sounded so splendidly desperate, the editor of the *Commentator* decided to print it, and, moreover, to see the authoress. He wrote, Would she care to see him, if he happened to be in her neighbourhood? He was going to lecture in Sheffield. She replied, Certainly.

He gave his afternoon lecture, on *Men In Books and Men in Life*. Naturally, men in books came first. Then he caught a train to reach the mining village where the Pinnegars lived.

It was February, with gruesome patches of snow. It was dark when he arrived at Mill Valley, a sort of thick, turgid darkness full of menace, where men speaking in a weird accent went past like ghosts, dragging their heavy feet and emitting the weird scent of the coalmine underworld. Weird and a bit gruesome it was.

He knew he had to walk uphill to the little market-place. As he went, he looked back and saw the black valleys with bunches of light, like camps of demons it seemed to him. And the demonish smell of sulphur and coal in the air, in the heavy, pregnant, clammy darkness.

They directed him to New London Lane, and down he went down another hill. His skin crept a little. The place felt uncanny and hostile, hard, as if iron and minerals breathed into the black air.

Thank goodness he couldn't see much, or be seen. When he had to ask his way the people treated him in a 'heave-half-a-brick-at-him' fashion.

After much weary walking and asking, he entered a lane between trees, in the cold slushy mud of the unfrozen February. The mines, apparently, were on the outskirts of the town, in some mud-sunk country. He could see the red, sore fires of the burning pit-hill through the trees, and he smelt the sulphur. He felt like some modern Ulysses wandering in the realms of Hecate. How much more dismal and horrible, a modern Odyssey among mines and factories, than any Sirens, Scyllas or Charybdises.

So he mused to himself as he waded through icy black mud, in a black lane, under black trees that moaned an accompaniment to the sound of the coalmine's occasional hissing and chuffing, under a black sky that quenched even the electric sparkle of the colliery. And the place seemed uninhabited like a cold black jungle.

At last he came in sight of a glimmer. Apparently, there were dwellings. Yes, a new little street, with one street-lamp, and the houses all apparently dark. He paused. Absolute desertion. Then three children.

They told him the house, and he stumbled up a dark passage. There was light on the little backyard. He knocked, in some trepidation. A rather tall woman, looking down at him with a 'Who are you?' look, from the step above.

'Mrs Pinnegar?'

'Oh, is it you, Mr Frith? Come in.'

He stumbled up the step into the glaring light of the kitchen. There stood Mrs Pinnegar, a tall woman with a face like a mask of passive anger, looking at him coldly. Immediately he felt his own shabbiness and smallness. In utter confusion, he stuck out his hand.

'I had an awful time getting here,' he said. 'I'm afraid I shall make a frightful mess of your house.' He looked down at his boots.

'That's all right,' she said. 'Have you had your tea?'

'No – but don't you bother about me.'

There was a little girl with fair hair in a fringe over her forehead, troubled blue eyes under the fringe, and two dolls. He felt easier.

'Is this your little girl?' he asked. 'She's awfully nice. What is her name?'

'Jane.'

'How are you, Jane?' he said. But the child only stared at him with the baffled, bewildered, pained eyes of a child who lives with hostile parents.

Mrs Pinnegar set his tea, bread and butter, jam, and buns. Then she sat opposite him. She was handsome, dark straight brows and grey eyes with yellow grains in them, and a way of looking straight at you as if she were used to holding her own. Her eyes were the nicest part of her. They had a certain kindliness, mingled, like the yellow grains among the grey, with a relentless, unyielding feminine will. Her nose and mouth were straight, like a Greek mask, and the expression was fixed. She gave him at once the impression of a woman who has made a mistake, who knows it, but who will not change: who cannot now change.

He felt very uneasy. Being a rather small, shambling man, she made him aware of his physical inconspicuousness. And she said not a word, only looked down on him, as he drank his tea, with that changeless look of a woman who is holding her own against Man and Fate. While, from the corner across the kitchen, the little girl with her fair hair and her dolls watched him also in absolute silence, from her hot blue eyes.

'This seems a pretty awful place,' he said to her.

'It is. It's absolutely awful,' the woman said.

'You ought to get away from it,' he said.

But she received this in dead silence.

It was exceedingly difficult to make any headway. He asked about Mr Pinnegar. She glanced at the clock.

'He comes up at nine,' she said.

'Is he down the mine?'

'Yes. He's on the afternoon shift.'

There was never a sound from the little girl.

'Doesn't Jane ever talk?' he asked.

'Not much,' said the mother, glancing round.

He talked a little about his lectures, about Sheffield, about London. But she was not really interested. She sat there rather distant, very laconic, looking at him with those curious unyielding eyes. She looked to him like a woman who has had her revenge, and is left

stranded on the reefs where she wrecked her
opponent. Still unrelenting, unregretting, unyielding, she seemed rather undecided as to what
her revenge had been, and what it had all been
about.

'You ought to get away from here,' he said to
her.

'Where to?' she asked.

'Oh' – he made a vague gesture – 'anywhere,
so long as it is *quite* away.'

She seemed to ponder this, under her portentous brow.

'I don't see what difference it would make,' she
said. Then glancing round at her child: 'I don't see
what difference anything would make, except
getting out of the world altogether. But there's
her to consider.' And she jerked her head in the
direction of the child.

Jimmy felt definitely frightened. He wasn't
used to this sort of grimness. At the same time
he was excited. This handsome, laconic woman,
with her soft brown hair and her unflinching eyes
with their gold flecks, seemed to be challenging
him to something. There was a touch of challenge
in her remaining gold-flecked kindness. Somewhere, she had a heart. But what had happened to
it? And why?

What had gone wrong with her? In some way,
she must have gone against herself.

'Why don't you come and live with me?' he
said, like the little gambler he was.

The queer, conflicting smile was on his face.

He had taken up her challenge, like a gambler. The very sense of a gamble, in which he could not lose desperately, excited him. At the same time, he was scared of her, and determined to get beyond his scare.

She sat and watched him, with the faintest touch of a grim smile on her handsome mouth.

'How do you mean, live with you?' she said.

'Oh – I mean what it usually means,' he said, with a little puff of self-conscious laughter.

'You're evidently not happy here. You're evidently in the wrong circumstances altogether. You're obviously *not* just an ordinary woman. Well, then, break away. When I say, Come and live with me, I mean just what I say. Come to London and live with me, as my wife, if you like, and then if we want to marry, when you get a divorce, why, we can do it.'

Jimmy made his speech more to himself than to the woman. That was how he was. He worked out all his things inside himself, as if it were all merely an interior problem of his own. And while he did so, he had an odd way of squinting his left eye and wagging his head loosely, like a man talking absolutely to himself, and turning his eyes inwards.

The woman watched him in a sort of wonder. This was something she was *not* used to. His extraordinary manner, and his extraordinary bald proposition, roused her from her own tense apathy.

'Well!' she said. 'That's got to be thought about. What about *her?*' – and again she jerked her head towards the round-eyed child in the corner. Jane sat with a completely expressionless face, her little red mouth fallen a little open. She seemed in a sort of trance: as if she understood like a grown-up person, but, as a child, sat in a trance, unconscious.

The mother wheeled round in her chair and stared at her child. The little girl stared back at her mother, with hot, troubled, almost guilty blue eyes. And neither said a word. Yet they seemed to exchange worlds of meaning.

'Why, of course,' said Jimmy, twisting his head again, 'she'd come, too.'

The woman gave a last look at her child, then turned to him, and started watching *him* with that slow, straight stare.

'It's not' – he began, stuttering – 'it's not anything *sudden* and unconsidered on my part. I've been considering it for quite a long time – ever since I had the first poem, and your letter.'

He spoke still with his eyes turned inwards, talking to himself. And the woman watched him unflinchingly.

'Before you ever saw me?' she asked, with a queer irony.

'Oh, of course. Of course before I ever saw you. Or else I never *should* have seen you. From the very first, I had a definite feeling—'

He made odd, sharp gestures, like a drunken man, and he spoke like a drunken man, his eyes turned inward, talking to himself. The woman was no more than a ghost moving inside his own consciousness, and he was addressing her there.

The actual woman sat outside looking on in a sort of wonder. This was really something new to her.

'And now you see me, do you want me, really, to come to London?'

She spoke in a dull tone of incredulity. The thing was just a little preposterous to her. But why not? It would have to be something a little preposterous, to get her out of the tomb she was in.

'Of course I do!' he cried, with another scoop of his head and scoop of his hand. '*Now* I do *actually* want you, now I actually see you.' He never looked at her. His eyes were still turned in. He was still talking to himself, in a sort of drunkenness with himself.

To her, it was something extraordinary. But it roused her from apathy.

He became aware of the hot blue eyes of the hot-cheeked little girl fixed upon him from the distant corner. And he gave a queer little giggle.

'Why, it's more than I could ever have hoped for,' he said, 'to have you and Jane live with me! Why, it will mean *life* to me.' He spoke in an odd, strained voice, slightly delirious. And for the first time he looked up at the woman and, apparently, *straight* at her. But, even as he seemed to look straight at her, the curious cast was in his eye, and he was only looking at himself, inside himself, at the shadows inside his own consciousness.

'And when would you like me to come?' she asked, rather coldly.

'Why, as soon as possible. Come back with me tomorrow, if you will. I've got a little house in St John's Wood, *waiting* for you. Come with me tomorrow. That's the simplest.'

She watched him for some time, as he sat with ducked head. He looked like a man who is drunk – drunk with himself. He was going bald at the crown, his rather curly black hair was thin.

'I couldn't come tomorrow, I should need a few days,' she said.

She wanted to see his face again. It was as if she could not remember what his face was like, this strange man who had appeared out of nowhere, with such a strange proposition.

He lifted his face, his eyes still cast in that inturned, blind look. He looked now like a Mephistopheles who has gone blind. With his black brows cocked up, Mephistopheles, Mephistopheles blind and begging in the street.

'Why, of course, it's wonderful that it's happened like this for me,' he said, with odd pouting emphasis, pushing out his lips. 'I was finished, absolutely finished. I was finished while Clarissa was with me. But after she'd gone, I was *absolutely* finished. And I thought there was no chance for me in the world again. It seems to me perfectly marvellous that this has happened – that I've come across you – ' he lifted his face sightlessly – 'and Jane – Jane – why she's *really* too good to be true.' He gave a slight hysterical laugh. 'She really is.'

The woman, and Jane, watched him with some embarrassment.

'I shall have to settle up here, with Mr Pinnegar,' she said, rather coldly musing. 'Do you want to see him?'

'Oh, I – ' he said, with a deprecating gesture, 'I don't *care*. But if you think I'd better – why, certainly – '

'I do think you'd better,' she said.

'Very well, then, I *will*. I'll see him whenever you like.'

'He comes in soon after nine,' she said.

'All right, I'll see him then. Much better. But I suppose I'd better see about finding a place to sleep first. Better not leave it too late.'

'I'll come with you and ask for you.'

'Oh, you'd better not, really. If you tell me where to go – '

He had taken on a protective tone: he was protecting her against herself and against scandal. It was his manner, his rather Oxfordy manner, more than anything else, that went beyond her. She wasn't used to it.

Jimmy plunged out into the gulfing blackness of the Northern night, feeling how horrible it was, but pressing his hat on his brow in a sense of strong adventure. He was going through with it.

At the baker's shop, where she had suggested he should ask for a bed, they would have none of him. Absolutely they didn't like the looks of him. At the Pub, too, they shook their heads: didn't want to have anything to do with him. But, in a voice more expostulatingly Oxford than ever, he said:

'But look here – you can't ask a man to sleep under one of these hedges. Can't I see the landlady?'

He persuaded the landlady to promise to let him sleep on the big, soft settee in the parlour, where the fire was burning brightly. Then, saying he would be back about ten, he returned through mud and drizzle up New London Lane.

The child was in bed, a saucepan was boiling by the fire. Already the lines had softened a little in the woman's face.

She spread a cloth on the table. Jimmy sat in silence, feeling that she was hardly aware of his presence. She was absorbed, no doubt, in the coming of her husband. The stranger merely sat on the sofa, and waited. He felt himself wound up tight. And once he was really wound up, he could go through with anything.

They heard the nine o'clock whistle at the mine. The woman then took the saucepan from the fire and went into the scullery. Jimmy could smell the smell of potatoes being strained. He sat quite still. There was nothing for him to do or say. He was wearing his big black-rimmed spectacles, and his face, blank and expressionless in the suspense of waiting, looked like the death-mask of some sceptical philosopher, who could wait through the ages, and who could hardly distinguish life from death at any time.

Came the heavy-shod tread up the house entry, and the man entered, rather like a blast of wind.

The fair moustache stuck out from the blackish, mottled face, and the fierce blue eyes rolled their whites in the coal-blackened sockets.

'This gentleman is Mr Frith,' said Emily Pinnegar.

Jimmy got up, with a bit of an Oxford wriggle, and held out his hand, saying: 'How do you do?'

His grey eyes, behind the spectacles, had an uncanny whitish gleam.

'My hand's not fit to shake hands,' said the miner. 'Take a seat.'

'Oh, nobody minds coal-dust,' said Jimmy, subsiding on to the sofa. 'It's clean dirt.'

'They say so,' said Pinnegar.

He was a man of medium height, thin, but energetic in build.

Mrs Pinnegar was running hot water into a pail from the bright brass tap of the stove, which had a boiler to balance the oven. Pinnegar dropped heavily into a wooden armchair, and stooped to pull off his ponderous grey pit-boots. He smelled of the strange, stale underground. In silence he pulled on his slippers, then rose, taking his boots into the scullery. His wife followed with the pail of hot water. She returned and spread a coarse roller-towel on the steel fender. The man could be heard washing in the scullery, in the semi-dark. Nobody said anything. Mrs Pinnegar attended to her husband's dinner.

After a while, Pinnegar came running in, naked to the waist, and squatted plumb in front of the big red fire, on his heels. His head and face and the

front part of his body were all wet. His back was
grey and unwashed. He seized the towel from the
fender and began to rub his face and head with a
sort of brutal vigour, while his wife brought a
bowl, and with a soapy flannel silently washed his
back, right down to the loins, where the trousers
were rolled back. The man was entirely oblivious
of the stranger – this washing was part of the
collier's ritual, and nobody existed for the moment. The woman, washing her husband's back,
stooping there as he kneeled with knees wide
apart, squatting on his heels on the rag hearthrug,
had a peculiar look on her strong, handsome face,
a look sinister and derisive. She was deriding
something or somebody; but Jimmy could not
make out whom or what.

It was a new experience for him to sit completely and brutally excluded, from a personal
ritual. The collier vigorously rubbed his own
fair short hair, till it all stood on end, then he
stared into the red-hot fire, oblivious, while the
red colour burned in his cheeks. Then again he
rubbed his breast and his body with the rough
towel, brutally, as if his body were some machine
he was cleaning, while his wife, with a peculiar
slow movement, dried his back with another
towel.

She took away the towel and bowl. The man
was dry. He still squatted with his hands on his
knees, gazing abstractedly, blankly into the fire.
That, too, seemed part of his daily ritual. The
colour flushed in his cheeks, his fair moustache

was rubbed on end. But his hot blue eyes stared hot and vague into the red coals, while the red glare of the coal fell on his breast and naked body.

He was a man of about thirty-five, in his prime, with a pure smooth skin and no fat on his body. His muscles were not large, but quick, alive with energy. And as he squatted bathing abstractedly in the glow of the fire, he seemed like some pure-moulded engine that sleeps between its motions, with incomprehensible eyes of dark iron-blue.

He looked round, always averting his face from the stranger on the sofa, shutting him out of consciousness. The wife took out a bundle from the dresser-cupboard, and handed it to the out-stretched, work-scarred hand of the man on the hearth. Curious, that big, horny, work-battered clean hand, at the end of the suave, thin naked arm.

Pinnegar unrolled his shirt and undervest in front of the fire, warmed them for a moment in the glow, vaguely, sleepily, then pulled them over his head. And then at last he rose, with his shirt hanging over his trousers, and in the same abstract, sleepy way, shutting the world out of his consciousness, he went out again to the scullery, pausing at the same dresser-cupboard to take out his rolled-up day trousers.

Mrs Pinnegar took away the towels and set the dinner on the table – rich, oniony stew out of a hissing brown stew-jar, boiled potatoes, and a cup of tea. The man returned from the scullery, in his clean flannelette shirt and black trousers, his fair hair neatly brushed. He planked his wooden armchair beside the table, and sat heavily down, to eat.

Then he looked at Jimmy, as one wary, probably hostile man looks at another.

"You're a stranger in these parts, I gather?' he said. There was something slightly formal, even a bit pompous, in his speech.

'An absolute stranger,' replied Jimmy, with a slight aside grin.

The man dabbed some mustard on his plate, and glanced at his food to see if he would like it.

'Come from a distance, do you?' he asked, as he began to eat. As he ate, he seemed to become oblivious again of Jimmy, bent his head over his plate, and ate. But probably he was ruminating something all the time, with barbaric wariness.

'From London,' said Jimmy warily.

'London!' said Pinnegar, without looking from his plate.

Mrs Pinnegar came and sat, in ritualistic silence, in her tall-backed rocking-chair under the light.

'What brings you this way, then?' asked Pinnegar, stirring his tea.

'Oh!' Jimmy writhed a little on the sofa. 'I came to see Mrs Pinnegar.'

The miner took a hasty gulp of tea.

'You're acquainted then, are you?' he said, still without looking round. He sat with his side-face to Jimmy.

'Yes, we are *now*,' explained Jimmy. 'I didn't know Mrs Pinnegar till this evening. As a matter of fact, she sent me some poems for the *Commentator* – I'm the editor – and I thought they were very good, so I wrote and told her so. Then I felt I wanted to come and see her, and she was willing, so I came.'

The man reached out, cut himself a piece of bread, and swallowed a large mouthful.

'You thought her poetry was good?' he said, turning at last to Jimmy and looking straight at him, with a stare something like the child's but aggressive. 'Are you going to put it in your magazine?'

'Yes, I think I am,' said Jimmy.

'I never read but one of her poems – something about a collier she knew all about, because she'd married him,' he said, in his peculiar harsh voice, that had a certain jeering clang in it, and a certain indomitableness.

Jimmy was silent. The other man's harsh fighting-voice made him shrink.

'I could never get on with the *Commentator* myself,' said Pinnegar, looking round for his pudding, pushing his meat-plate aside. 'Seems to me to go a long way round to get nowhere.'

'Well, probably it *does*,' said Jimmy, squirming a little. 'But so long as the *way* is interesting! I don't see that anything gets anywhere at present – certainly no periodical.'

'I don't know,' said Pinnegar. 'There's some facts in the *Liberator* – and there's some ideas in the *Janus*. I can't see the use, myself, of all these feelings folk say they have. They get you nowhere.'

'But,' said Jimmy, with a slight pouf of laughter, 'where do you *want* to get? It's all very well talking about getting somewhere, but where, where in the world today do you *want* to get? In general, I mean. If you want a better job in the mine – all right, go ahead and get it. But when you begin to talk about getting somewhere, in *life* – why, you've got to know what you're talking about.'

'I'm a man, aren't I?' said the miner, going very still and hard.

'But what do you *mean*, when you say you're a man?' snarled Jimmy, really exasperated. 'What do you mean? Yes, you *are* a man. But what about it?'

'Haven't I the right to say I won't be made use of?' said the collier, slow, harsh, and heavy.

'You've got a right to *say* it,' retorted Jimmy, with a pouf of laughter. 'But it doesn't *mean* anything. We're all made use of, from King George downwards. We have to be. When you eat your pudding you're making use of hundreds of people – including your wife.'

'I know it. I know it. It makes no difference, though. I'm not going to be made use of.'

Jimmy shrugged his shoulders.

'Oh, all right!' he said. 'That's just a phrase, like any other.'

The miner sat very still in his chair, his face going hard and remote. He was evidently thinking over something that was stuck like a barb in his consciousness, something he was trying to harden over, as the skin sometimes hardens over a steel splinter in the flesh.

'I'm nothing but made use of,' he said, now talking hard and final, to himself, and staring out into space. 'Down the pit, I'm made use of, and they give me a wage, such as it is. At the house, I'm made use of, and my wife sets the dinner on the table as if I was a customer in a shop.'

'But what do you *expect?*' cried Jimmy, writhing in his chair.

'Me? What do I expect? I expect nothing. But I tell you what – ' he turned, and looked straight and hard into Jimmy's eyes – 'I'm not going to put up with anything either.'

Jimmy saw the hard finality in the other man's eyes, and squirmed away from it.

'If you *know* what you're not going to put up with – ' he said.

'I don't want my wife writing poetry! And sending it to a parcel of men she's never seen. *I* don't want my wife sitting like Queen Boadicea, when I come home, and a face like a stone wall with holes in it. I don't know what's wrong with her. She doesn't know herself. But she does as she likes. Only, mark you, I do the same.'

'Of course!' cried Jimmy, though there was no of course about it.

'She's told you I've got another woman?'

'Yes.'

'And I'll tell you for why. If I give in to the coal face, and go down the mine every day to eight hours' slavery, more or less, somebody's got to give in to me.'

'Then,' said Jimmy, after a pause, 'if you mean you want your wife to submit to you – well, that's the problem. You have to marry the woman who *will* submit.'

It was amazing, this from Jimmy. He sat there and lectured the collier like a Puritan Father, completely forgetting the disintegrating flutter of Clarissa, in his own background.

'I want a wife who'll please me, who'll want to please me,' said the collier.

'Why should *you* be pleased, any more than anybody else?' asked the wife coldly.

'My child, my little girl wants to please me – if her mother would let her. But the women hang together. I tell you' – and here he turned to Jimmy, with a blaze in his dark blue eyes – 'I want a woman to please me, a woman who's anxious to please me. And if I can't find her in my own home, I'll find her out of it.'

'I hope she pleases you,' said the wife, rocking slightly.

'Well,' said the man, 'she does.'

'Then why don't you go and live with her altogether?' she said.

He turned and looked at her.

'Why don't I?' he said. 'Because I've got my home. I've got my house, I've got my wife, let her be what she may, as a woman to live with. And I've got my child. Why should I break it all up?'

'And what about me?' she asked, coldly and fiercely.

'You? You've got a home. You've got a child. You've got a man who works for you. You've got what you want. You do as you like – '

'Do I?' she asked, with intolerable sarcasm.

'Yes. Apart from the bit of work in the house, you do as you like. If you want to go, you can go. But while you live in my house, you must respect it. You bring no men here, you see.'

'Do *you* respect your home?' she said.

'Yes! I do! If I get another woman – who pleases me – I deprive you of nothing. All I ask of you is to do your duty as a housewife.'

'Down to washing your back!' she said, heavily sarcastic; and, Jimmy thought, a trifle vulgar.

'Down to washing my back, since it's got to be washed,' he said.

'What about the other woman? Let her do it.'

'This is my home.'

The wife gave a strange movement, like a mad woman.

Jimmy sat rather pale and frightened. Behind the collier's quietness he felt the concentration of almost cold anger and an unchanging will. In the man's lean face he could see the bones, the fixity of the male bones, and it was as if the human soul, or spirit, had gone into the living skull and skeleton, almost invulnerable.

Jimmy, for some strange reason, felt a wild anger against this bony and logical man. It was the hard-driven coldness, fixity, that he could not bear.

'Look here!' he cried, in a resonant Oxford voice, his eyes glaring and casting inwards behind his spectacles. 'You say Mrs Pinnegar is *free* – free to do as she pleases. In that case you have no objection if she comes with me right away from here.'

The collier looked at the pale, strange face of the editor in wonder. Jimmy kept his face slightly averted, and sightless, seeing nobody. There was a Mephistophelian tilt about the eyebrows, and a Martyred Sebastian straightness about the mouth.

'Does she *want* to?' asked Pinnegar, with devastating incredulity. The wife smiled faintly, grimly. She could see the vanity of her husband in his utter inability to believe that she could prefer the other man to him.

'That,' said Jimmy, 'you must ask her yourself. But it's what I came here for: to ask her to come and live with me, and bring the child.'

'You came without having seen her, to ask her that?' said the husband, in growing wonder.

'Yes,' said Jimmy, vehemently, nodding his head with drunken emphasis. 'Yes! Without ever having seen her!'

'You've caught a funny fish this time, with your poetry,' he said, turning with curious husband-familiarity to his wife. She hated this off-hand husband-familiarity.

'What sort of fish have *you* caught?' she retorted. 'And what did you catch *her* with?'

'Bird-lime!' he said, with a faint, quick grin.

Jimmy was sitting in suspense. They all three sat in suspense, for some time.

'And what are you saying to him?' said the collier at length.

Jimmy looked up, and the malevolent half-smile on his face made him look rather handsome again, a mixture of faun and Mephisto. He glanced curiously, invitingly, at the woman who was watching him from afar.

'I say yes!' she replied, in a cool voice.

The husband became very still, sitting erect in his wooden armchair and staring into space. It was as if he were fixedly watching something fly away from him, out of his own soul. But he was not going to yield at all, to any emotion.

He could not now believe that this woman should *want* to leave him. Yet she did.

'I'm sure it's all for the best,' said Jimmy, in his Puritan-Father voice. 'You don't mind, really' – he drawled uneasily – 'if she brings the child. I give you my word I'll do my very best for it.'

The collier looked at him as if he were very far away. Jimmy quailed under the look. He could see that the other man was relentlessly killing the emotion in himself, stripping himself, as it were, of his own flesh, stripping himself to the hard unemotional bone of the human male.

'I give her a blank cheque,' said Pinnegar, with numb lips. 'She does as she pleases.'

'So much for fatherly love, compared with selfishness,' she said.

He turned and looked at her with that curious power of remote anger. And immediately she became still, quenched.

'I give you a blank cheque, as far as I'm concerned,' he repeated abstractedly.

'It *is* blank indeed!' she said, with her first touch of bitterness.

Jimmy looked at the clock. It was growing late: he might be shut out of the public-house. He rose to go, saying he would return in the morning. He was leaving the next day, at noon, for London.

He plunged into the darkness and mud of that black, night-ridden country. There was a curious elation in his spirits, mingled with fear. But then he always needed an element of fear, really, to elate him. He thought with terror of those two human beings left in that house together. The frightening state of tension! He himself could never bear an extreme tension. He always had to compromise, to become apologetic and pathetic. He would be able to manage Mrs Pinnegar that way. Emily! He must get used to saying it. Emily! The Emilia was absurd. He had never known an Emily.

He felt really scared, and really elated. He was doing something big. It was not that he was in *love* with the woman. But, my God, he wanted to take her away from that man. And he wanted the adventure of her. Absolutely the adventure of her. He felt really elated, really himself, really manly.

But in the morning he returned rather sheepishly to the collier's house. It was another dark, drizzling day, with black trees, black road, black hedges, blackish brick houses, and the smell and the sound of collieries under a skyless day. Like living in some weird underground.

Unwillingly he went up that passage-entry again, and knocked at the back door, glancing at the miserable little back garden with its cabbage-stalks and its ugly sanitary arrangements.

The child opened the door to him: with her fair hair, flushed cheeks, and hot, dark-blue eyes.

'Hello, Jane!' he said.

The mother stood tall and square, by the table, watching him with portentous eyes, as he entered. She was handsome, but her skin was not very good: as if the battle had been too much for her health. Jimmy glanced up at her smiling his slow, ingratiating smile, that always brought a glow of success into a woman's spirit. And as he saw her gold-flecked eyes searching in his eyes, without a bit of kindliness, he thought to himself: 'My God, however am I going to sleep with that woman!' His will was ready, however, and he would manage it somehow.

And when he glanced at the motionless, bony head and lean figure of the collier seated in the wooden armchair by the fire, he was more ready. He must triumph over that man.

'What train are you going by?' asked Mrs Pinnegar.

'By the twelve-thirty.' He looked up at her as he spoke, with the wide, shining, childlike, almost coy eyes that were his peculiar asset. She looked

down at him in a sort of interested wonder. She
seemed almost fascinated by his childlike, shining,
inviting dark-grey eyes, with their long lashes:
such an absolute change from that resentful
unyielding that looked out always from the back
of her husband's blue eyes. Her husband always
seemed like a menace to her, in his thinness, his
concentration, his eternal unyielding. And this man
looked at one with the wide, shining, fascinating
eyes of a young Persian kitten, something at once
bold and shy and coy and strangely inviting. She fell
at once under their spell.

'You'll have dinner before you go,' she said.

'No!' he cried in panic, unwilling indeed to eat
before that other man. 'No, I ate a fabulous
breakfast. I will get a sandwich when I change
in Sheffield: *really!*'

She had to go out shopping. She said she would
go out to the station with him when she got back.
It was just after eleven.

'But look here,' he said, addressing also the thin
abstracted man who sat unnoticing, with a newspaper, 'we've got to get this thing settled. I *want*
Mrs Pinnegar to come and live with me, her and
the child. And she's coming! So don't you think,
now, it would be better if she came right along
with me today! Just put a few things in a bag and
come along. Why drag the thing out?'

'I tell you,' replied the husband, 'she has a blank
cheque from me to do as she likes.'

'All right, then! Won't you do that? Won't you
come along with me now?' said Jimmy, looking

up at her exposedly, but casting his eyes a bit inwards. Throwing himself with deliberate impulsiveness on her mercy.

'I can't!' she said decisively. 'I can't come today.'

'But why not – really? Why not, while I'm here? You have the blank cheque, you can do as you please – '

'The blank cheque won't get me far,' she said rudely. 'I can't come today, anyhow.'

'When can you come, then?' he said, with that queer, petulant pleading. 'The sooner the better, surely.'

'I can come on Monday,' she said abruptly.

'Monday!' He gazed up at her in a kind of panic, through his spectacles. Then he set his teeth again, and nodded his head up and down. 'All right, then! Today is Saturday. Then Monday!'

'If you'll excuse me,' she said, 'I've got to go out for a few things. I'll walk to the station with you when I get back.'

She bundled Jane into a little sky-blue coat and bonnet, put on a heavy black coat and black hat herself, and went out.

Jimmy sat very uneasily opposite the collier, who also wore spectacles to read. Pinnegar put down the newspaper and pulled the spectacles off his nose, saying something about a Labour Government.

'Yes,' said Jimmy. 'After all, best be logical. If you *are* democratic, the only logical thing is a Labour Government. Though, personally, one Government is as good as another, to me.'

'Maybe so!' said the collier. 'But *something's* got to come to an end, sooner or later.'

'Oh, a great deal!' said Jimmy, and they lapsed into silence.

'Have you been married before?' asked Pinnegar, at length.

'Yes. My wife and I are divorced.'

'I suppose you want me to divorce *my* wife?' said the collier.

'Why – yes! – that would be best – '

'It's the same to me,' said Pinnegar; 'divorce or no divorce. I'll *live* with another woman, but I'll never *marry* another. Enough is as good as a feast. But if she wants a divorce, she can have it.'

'It would certainly be best,' said Jimmy.

There was a long pause. Jimmy wished the woman would come back.

'I look on you as an instrument,' said the miner. 'Something had to break. You are the instrument that breaks it.'

It was strange to sit in the room with this thin, remote, wilful man. Jimmy was a bit fascinated by him. But, at the same time, he hated him because he could not be in the same room with him without being under his spell. He felt himself dominated. And he hated it.

'My wife,' said Pinnegar, looking up at Jimmy with a peculiar, almost humorous, teasing grin, 'expects to see me go to the dogs when she leaves me. It is her last hope.'

Jimmy ducked his head and was silent, not knowing what to say. The other man sat still in his chair, like a sort of infinitely patient prisoner, looking away out of the window and waiting.

'She thinks,' he said again, 'that she has some wonderful future awaiting her somewhere, and you're going to open the door.'

And again the same amused grin was in his eyes.

And again Jimmy was fascinated by the man. And again he hated the spell of this fascination. For Jimmy wanted to be, in his own mind, the strongest man among men, but particularly among women. And this thin, peculiar man could dominate him. He knew it. The very silent unconsciousness of Pinnegar dominated the room, wherever he was.

Jimmy hated this.

At last Mrs Pinnegar came back, and Jimmy set off with her. He shook hands with the collier.

'Goodbye!' he said.

'Goodbye!' said Pinnegar, looking down at him with those amused blue eyes, which Jimmy knew he would never be able to get beyond.

And the walk to the station was almost a walk of conspiracy against the man left behind, between the man in spectacles and the tall woman. They arranged the details for Monday. Emily was to come by the nine o'clock train: Jimmy would meet her at Marylebone, and install her in his house in St John's Wood. Then, with the child, they would begin a new life. Pinnegar would divorce his wife, or she would divorce him: and then, another marriage.

Jimmy got a tremendous kick out of it all on the journey home. He felt he had really done something desperate and adventurous. But he was in too wild a flutter to analyse any results. Only, as he drew near London, a sinking feeling came over him. He was desperately tired after it all, almost too tired to keep up.

Nevertheless, he went after dinner and sprang it all on Severn.

'You damn fool!' said Severn, in consternation. 'What did you do it for?'

'Well,' said Jimmy, writhing. 'Because *I wanted* to.'

'Good God! The woman sounds like the head of Medusa. You're a hero of some stomach, I must say! Remember Clarissa?'

'Oh,' writhed Jimmy. 'But this is different.'

'Ay, her name's Emma, or something of that sort, isn't it?'

'Emily!' said Jimmy briefly.

'Well, you're a fool, anyway, so you may as well keep on acting in character. I've no doubt, by playing weeping willow, you'll outlive all the female storms you ever prepare for yourself. I never yet did see a weeping willow uprooted by a gale, so keep on hanging your harp on it, and you'll be all right. Here's luck! But for a man who was looking for a little Gretchen to adore him, you're a corker!'

Which was all that Severn had to say. But Jimmy went home with his knees shaking. On Sunday morning he wrote an anxious letter. He didn't know how to begin it: *Dear Mrs Pinnegar* and *Dear Emily* seemed either too late in the day or too early. So he just plunged in, without dear anything.

'I want you to have this before you come. Perhaps we have been precipitate. I only beg you to decide *finally*, for yourself, before you come. Don't come, please, unless you are absolutely sure of yourself. If you are *in the least* unsure, wait a while, wait till you are quite certain, one way or the other.

'For myself, if you don't come I shall understand. But please send me a telegram. If you do come, I shall welcome both you and the child. Yours ever – J.F.'

He paid a man his return fare, and three pounds extra, to go on the Sunday and deliver this letter.

The man came back in the evening. He had delivered the letter. There was no answer.

Awful Sunday night: tense Monday morning!

A telegram: *Arrive Marylebone 12.50 with Jane. Yours ever. Emily.*

Jimmy set his teeth and went to the station. But when he felt her looking at him, and so met her eyes: and after that saw her coming slowly down the platform, holding the child by the hand, her slow cat's eyes smouldering under her straight brows, smouldering at him: he almost swooned. A sickly grin came over him as he held out his hand. Nevertheless he said:

'I'm *awfully* glad you came.'

And he sat in the taxi, a perverse but intense desire for her came over him, making him almost helpless. He could feel, so strongly, the presence of that other man about her, and this went to his head like neat spirits. That other man! In some subtle, inexplicable way, he was actually bodily present, the husband. The woman moved in his aura. She was hopelessly married to him.

And this went to Jimmy's head like neat whisky. Which of the two would fall before him with a greater fall – the woman or the man, her husband?

The Woman Who Rode Away

She had thought that this marriage, of all marriages, would be an adventure. Not that the man himself was exactly magical to her. A little, wiry, twisted fellow, twenty years older than herself, with brown eyes and greying hair, who had come to America a scrap of a wastrel, from Holland, years ago, as a tiny boy, and from the gold-mines of the west had been kicked south into Mexico, and now was more or less rich, owning silver-mines in the wilds of the Sierra Madre: it was obvious that the adventure lay in his circumstances, rather than his person. But he was still a little dynamo of energy, in spite of accidents survived, and what he had accomplished he had accomplished alone. One of those human oddments there is no accounting for.

When she actually *saw* what he had accomplished, her heart quailed. Great green-covered, unbroken mountain-hills, and in the midst of the lifeless isolation, the sharp pinkish mounds of the dried mud from the silver-works. Under the nakedness of the works, the walled-in, one-storey adobe house, with its garden inside, and its deep inner verandah with tropical climbers on the sides. And when you looked up from this shut-in flowered patio, you saw the huge pink cone of the silver-mud refuse, and the machinery of the extracting plant against heaven above. No more.

To be sure, the great wooden doors were often open. And then she could stand outside, in the vast open world. And see great, void, tree-clad hills piling behind one another, from nowhere into nowhere. They were green in autumn time. For the rest, pinkish, stark dry, and abstract.

And in his battered Ford car her husband would take her into the dead, thrice-dead little Spanish town forgotten among the mountains. The great, sun-dried dead church, the dead portales, the hopeless covered market-place, where, the first time she went, she saw a dead dog lying between the meat stalls and the vegetable array, stretched out as if for ever, nobody troubling to throw it away. Deadness within deadness.

Everybody feebly talking silver, and showing bits of ore. But silver was at a standstill. The great war came and went. Silver was a dead market. Her husband's mines were closed down. But she and he lived on in the adobe house under the works, among the flowers that were never very flowery to her.

She had two children, a boy and a girl. And her eldest, the boy, was nearly ten years old before she aroused from her stupor of subjected amazement. She was now thirty-three, a large, blue-eyed, dazed woman, beginning to grow stout. Her little, wiry, tough, twisted, brown-eyed husband was fifty-three, a man as tough as wire, tenacious as wire, still full of energy, but dimmed by the lapse of silver from the market, and by some curious inaccessibility on his wife's part.

He was a man of principles, and a good husband. In a way, he doted on her. He never quite got over his dazzled admiration of her. But essentially, he was still a bachelor. He had been thrown out on the world, a little bachelor, at the age of ten. When he married he was over forty, and had enough money to marry on. But his capital was all a bachelor's. He was boss of his own works, and marriage was the last and most intimate bit of his own works.

He admired his wife to extinction, he admired her body, all her points. And she was to him always the rather dazzling Californian girl from Berkeley, whom he had first known. Like any sheik, he kept her guarded among those mountains of Chihuahua. He was jealous of her as he was of his silver-mine: and that is saying a lot.

At thirty-three she really was still the girl from Berkeley, in all but physique. Her conscious development had stopped mysteriously with her marriage, completely arrested. Her husband had never become real to her, neither mentally nor physically. In spite of his late sort of passion for her, he never meant anything to her, physically. Only morally he swayed her, downed her, kept her in an invincible slavery.

So the years went by, in the adobe house strung round the sunny patio, with the silver-works overhead. Her husband was never still. When the silver went dead, he ran a ranch lower down, some twenty miles away, and raised pure-bred hogs, splendid creatures. At the same time, he hated pigs. He was a squeamish waif of an idealist, and really hated the physical side of life. He loved work, work, work, and making things. His marriage, his children, were something he was making, part of his business, but with a sentimental income this time.

Gradually her nerves began to go wrong: she must get out. She must get out. So he took her to El Paso for three months. And at least it was the United States.

But he kept his spell over her. The three months ended: back she was, just the same, in her adobe house among those eternal green or pinky-brown hills, void as only the undiscovered is void. She taught her children, she supervised the Mexican boys who were her servants. And sometimes her husband brought visitors, Spaniards or Mexicans or occasionally white men.

He really loved to have white men staying on the place. Yet he had not a moment's peace when they were there. It was as if his wife were some peculiar secret vein of ore in his mines, which no one must be aware of except himself. And she was fascinated by the young gentlemen, mining engineers, who were his guests at times. He, too, was fascinated by a real gentleman. But he was an old-timer miner with a wife, and if a gentleman looked at his wife, he felt as if his mine were being looted, the secrets of it pryed out.

It was one of these young gentlemen who put the idea into her mind. They were all standing outside the great wooden doors of the patio, looking at the outer world. The eternal, motionless hills were all green, it was September, after the rains. There was no sign of anything, save the deserted mine, the deserted works, and a bunch of half-deserted miners' dwellings.

'I wonder,' said the young man, 'what there is behind those great blank hills.'

'More hills,' said Lederman. 'If you go that way, Sonora and the coast. This way is the desert – you came from there. – And the other way, hills and mountains.'

'Yes, but what *lives* in the hills and the mountains? *Surely* there is something wonderful? It looks *so* like nowhere on earth: like being on the moon.'

'There's plenty of game, if you want to shoot. And Indians, if you call *them* wonderful.'

'Wild ones?'

'Wild enough.'

'But friendly?'

'It depends. Some of them are quite wild, and they don't let anybody near. They kill a missionary at sight. And where a missionary can't get, nobody can.'

'But what does the government say?'

'They're so far from everywhere, the government leaves 'em alone. And they're wily; if they think there'll be trouble, they send a delegation to Chihuahua and make a formal submission. The government is glad to leave it at that.'

'And do they live quite wild, with their own savage customs and religion?'

'Oh, yes. They use nothing but bows and arrows. I've seen them in town, in the Plaza, with funny sort of hats with flowers round them, and a bow in one hand, quite naked except for a sort of shirt, even in cold weather – striding round with their savage's bare legs.'

'But don't you suppose it's wonderful, up there in their secret villages?'

'No. What would there be wonderful about it? Savages are savages, and all savages behave more or less alike: rather low-down and dirty, insanitary, with a few cunning tricks, and struggling to get enough to eat.'

'But surely they have old, old religions and mysteries – it *must* be wonderful, surely it must.'

'I don't know about mysteries – howling and heathen practices, more or less indecent. No, I see nothing wonderful in that kind of stuff. And I wonder that you should, when you have lived in London or Paris or New York – '

'Ah, *everybody* lives in London or Paris or New York' – said the young man, as if this were an argument.

And his peculiar vague enthusiasm for unknown Indians found a full echo in the woman's heart. She was overcome by a foolish romanticism more unreal than a girl's. She felt it was her destiny to wander into the secret haunts of these timeless, mysterious, marvellous Indians of the mountains.

She kept her secret. The young man was departing, her husband was going with him down to Torreon, on business: – would be away for some days. But before the departure, she made her husband talk about the Indians: about the wandering tribes, resembling the Navajo, who were still wandering free; and the Yaquis of Sonora: and the different groups in the different valleys of Chihuahua State.

There was supposed to be one tribe, the Chilchuis, living in a high valley to the south, who were the sacred tribe of all the Indians. The descendants of Montezuma and of the old Aztec or Totonac kings still lived among them, and the old priests still kept up the ancient religion, and offered human sacrifices – so it was said. Some scientists had been to the Chilchui country, and had come back gaunt and exhausted with hunger and bitter privation, bringing various curious, barbaric objects of worship, but having seen nothing extraordinary in the hungry, stark village of savages.

Though Lederman talked in this off-hand way, it was obvious he felt some of the vulgar excitement at the idea of ancient and mysterious savages.

'How far away are they?' she asked.

'Oh – three days on horseback – past Cuchitee and a little lake there is up there.'

Her husband and the young man departed. The woman made her crazy plans. Of late, to break the monotony of her life, she had harassed her husband into letting her go riding with him, occasionally, on horseback. She was never allowed to go out alone. The country truly was not safe, lawless and crude.

But she had her own horse, and she dreamed of being free as she had been as a girl, among the hills of California.

Her daughter, nine years old, was now in a tiny convent in the little half-deserted Spanish mining-town five miles away.

'Manuel,' said the woman to her house-servant, 'I'm going to ride to the convent to see Margarita, and take her a few things. Perhaps I shall stay the night in the convent. You look after Freddy and see everything is all right till I come back.'

'Shall I ride with you on the master's horse, or shall Juan?' asked the servant.

'Neither of you. I shall go alone.'

The young man looked her in the eyes, in protest. Absolutely impossible that the woman should ride alone!

'I shall go alone,' repeated the large, placid-seeming, fair-complexioned woman, with peculiar overbearing emphasis. And the man silently, unhappily yielded.

'Why are you going alone, mother?' asked her son, as she made up parcels of food.

'Am I *never* to be let alone? Not one moment of my life?' she cried, with sudden explosion of energy. And the child, like the servant, shrank into silence.

She set off without a qualm, riding astride on her strong roan horse, and wearing a riding suit of coarse linen, a riding skirt over her linen breeches, a scarlet neck-tie over her white blouse, and a black felt hat on her head. She had food in her saddle-bags, an army canteen with water, and a large, native blanket tied on behind the saddle. Peering into the distance, she set off from her home. Manuel and the little boy stood in the gateway to watch her go. She did not even turn to wave them farewell.

But when she had ridden about a mile, she left the wild road and took a small trail to the right, that led into another valley, over steep places and past great trees, and through another deserted mining-settlement. It was September, the water was running freely in the little stream that had fed the now-abandoned mine. She got down to drink, and let the horse drink too.

She saw natives coming through the trees, away up the slope. They had seen her, and were watching her closely. She watched in turn. The three people, two women and a youth, were making a wide detour, so as not to come too close to her. She did not care. Mounting, she trotted ahead up the silent valley, beyond the silver-works, beyond any trace of mining. There was still a rough trail, that led over rocks and loose stones into the valley beyond. This trail she had already ridden, with her husband. Beyond that she knew she must go south.

Curiously she was not afraid, although it was a frightening country, the silent, fatal-seeming mountain slopes, the occasional distant, suspicious, elusive natives among the trees, the great carrion birds occasionally hovering, like great flies, in the distance, over some carrion or some ranch house or some group of huts.

As she climbed, the trees shrank and the trail ran through a thorny scrub, that was trailed over with blue convolvulus and an occasional pink creeper. Then these flowers lapsed. She was nearing the pine trees.

She was over the crest, and before her another silent, void, green-clad valley. It was past midday. Her horse turned to a little runlet of water, so she got down to eat her midday meal. She sat in silence looking at the motionless unliving valley, and at the sharp-peaked hills, rising higher to rock and pine trees, southwards. She rested two hours in the heat of the day, while the horse cropped around her.

Curious that she was neither afraid nor lonely. Indeed, the loneliness was like a drink of cold water to one who is very thirsty. And a strange elation sustained her from within.

She travelled on, and camped at night in a valley beside a stream, deep among the bushes. She had seen cattle and had crossed several trails. There must be a ranch not far off. She heard the strange wailing shriek of a mountain lion, and the answer of dogs. But she sat by her small camp fire in a secret hollow place and was not really afraid. She was buoyed up always by the curious, bubbling elation within her.

It was very cold before dawn. She lay wrapped in her blanket looking at the stars, listening to her horse shivering, and feeling like a woman who has died and passed beyond. She was not sure that she had not heard, during the night, a great crash at the centre of herself, which was the crash of her own death. Or else it was a crash at the centre of the earth, and meant something big and mysterious.

With the first peep of light she got up, numb with cold, and made a fire. She ate hastily, gave her horse some pieces of oil-seed cake, and set off again. She avoided any meeting – and since she met nobody, it was evident that she in turn was avoided. She came at last in sight of the village of Cuchitee, with its black houses with their reddish roofs, a sombre, dreary little cluster below another silent, long-abandoned mine. And beyond, a long, great mountainside, rising up green and light to the darker, shaggier green of pine trees. And beyond the pine trees stretches of naked rock against the sky, rock slashed already and brindled with white stripes of snow. High up, the new snow had already begun to fall.

And now, as she neared, more or less, her destination, she began to go vague and disheartened. She had passed the little lake among yellow aspen trees whose white trunks were round and suave like the white round arms of some woman. What a lovely place! In California she would have raved about it. But here she looked and saw that it was lovely, but she didn't care. She was weary and spent with her two nights in the open, and afraid of the coming night. She didn't know where she was going, or what she was going for. Her horse plodded dejectedly on, towards that immense and forbidding mountain-slope, following a stony little trail. And if she had had any will of her own left, she would have turned back, to the village, to be protected and sent home to her husband.

But she had no will of her own. Her horse splashed through a brook, and turned up a valley, under immense yellowing cottonwood trees. She must have been near nine thousand feet above sea-level, and her head was light with the altitude and with weariness. Beyond the cottonwood trees she could see, on each side, the steep sides of mountain slopes hemming her in, sharp-plumaged with overlapping aspen, and, higher up, with sprouting, pointed spruce and pine tree. Her horse went on automatically. In this tight valley, on this slight trail, there was nowhere to go but ahead, climbing.

Suddenly her horse jumped, and three men in dark blankets were on the trail before her.

'*Adiós*,' came the greeting, in the full, restrained Indian voice.

'*Adiós!*' she replied, in her assured, American woman's voice.

'Where are you going?' came the quiet question, in Spanish.

The men in the dark sarapes had come closer, and were looking up at her.

'On ahead,' she replied coolly, in her hard, Saxon Spanish.

These were just natives to her: dark-faced, strongly-built men in dark sarapes and straw hats. They would have been the same as the men who worked for her husband, except, strangely, for the long black hair that fell over their shoulders. She noted this long black hair with a certain distaste. These must the wild Indians she had come to see.

'Where do you come from?' the same man asked. It was always the one man who spoke. He was young, with quick, large, bright black eyes that glanced sideways at her. He had a soft black moustache on his dark face, and a sparse tuft of beard, loose hairs on his chin. His long black hair, full of life, hung unrestrained on his shoulders. Dark as he was, he did not look as if he had washed lately.

His two companions were the same, but older men, powerful and silent. One had a thin black line of moustache, but was beardless. The other had the smooth cheeks and the sparse dark hairs marking the lines of his chin with the beard characteristic of the Indians.

'I come from far away,' she replied, with half-jocular evasion.

This was received in silence.

'But where do you live?' asked the young man, with that same quiet insistence.

'In the north,' she replied airily.

Again there was a moment's silence. The young man conversed quietly in Indian, with his two companions.

'Where do you want to go, up this way?' he asked suddenly, with challenge and authority, pointing briefly up the trail.

'To the Chilchui Indians,' answered the woman laconically.

The young man looked at her. His eyes were quick and black, and inhuman. He saw, in the full evening light, the faint sub-smile of assurance on her rather large, calm, fresh-complexioned face; the weary, bluish lines under her large blue eyes; and in her eyes, as she looked down at him, a half-childish, half-arrogant confidence in her own female power. But in her eyes, also, a curious look of trance.

'*Usted es Señora?* You are a lady?' the Indian asked her.

'Yes, I am a lady,' she replied complacently.

'With a family?'

'With a husband and two children, boy and girl,' she said.

The Indian turned to his companions and translated, in the low, gurgling speech, like hidden water running. They were evidently at a loss.

'Where is your husband?' asked the young man.

'Who knows?' she replied airily. 'He has gone away on business for a week.'

The black eyes watched her shrewdly. She, for all her weariness, smiled faintly in the pride of her own adventure and the assurance of her own womanhood, and the spell of the madness that was on her.

'And what do *you* want to do?' the Indian asked her.

'I want to visit the Chilchui Indians – to see their houses and to know their gods,' she replied.

The young man turned and translated quickly, and there was a silence almost of consternation. The grave elder men were glancing at her sideways, with strange looks, from under their decorated hats. And they said something to the young man, in deep chest voices.

The latter still hesitated. Then he turned to the woman.

'Good!' he said. 'Let us go. But we cannot arrive until tomorrow. We shall have to make camp tonight.'

'Good!' she said. 'I can make a camp.'

Without more ado, they set off at a good speed up the stony trail. The young Indian ran alongside her horse's head, the other two ran behind. One of them had taken a thick stick, and occasionally he struck her horse a resounding blow on the haunch, to urge him forward. This made the horse jump, and threw her back in the saddle, which, tired as she was, made her angry.

'Don't do that!' she cried, looking round angrily at the fellow. She met his black, large, bright eyes, and for the first time her spirit really quailed. The man's eyes were not human to her, and they did not see her as a beautiful white woman. He looked at her with a black, bright inhuman look, and saw no woman in her at all. As if she were some strange, unaccountable *thing*, incomprehensible to him, but inimical. She sat in her saddle in wonder, feeling once more as if she had died. And again he struck her horse, and jerked her badly in the saddle.

All the passionate anger of the spoilt white woman rose in her. She pulled her horse to a standstill, and turned with blazing eyes to the man at her bridle.

'Tell that fellow not to touch my horse again,' she cried.

She met the eyes of the young man, and in their bright black inscrutability she saw a fine spark, as in a snake's eye, of derision. He spoke to his companion in the rear, in the low tones of the Indian. The man with the stick listened without looking. Then, giving a strange low cry to the horse, he struck it again on the rear, so that it leaped forward spasmodically up the stony trail, scattering the stones, pitching the weary woman in her seat.

The anger flew like a madness into her eyes, she went white at the gills. Fiercely she reined in her horse. But before she could turn, the young Indian had caught the reins under the horse's throat, jerked them forward, and was trotting ahead rapidly, leading the horse.

The woman was powerless. And along with her supreme anger there came a slight thrill of exultation. She knew she was dead.

The sun was setting, a great yellow light flooded the last of the aspens, flared on the trunks of the pine trees, the pine-needles bristled and stood out with dark lustre, the rocks glowed with unearthly glamour. And through this effulgence the Indian at her horse's head trotted unweariedly on, his dark blanket swinging, his bare legs glowing with a strange transfigured ruddiness in the powerful light, and his straw hat with its half-absurd decorations of flowers and feathers shining showily above his river of long black hair. At times he would utter a low call to the horse, and then the other Indians, behind, would fetch the beast a whack with the stick.

The wonder-light faded off the mountains, the world began to grow dark, a cold air breathed down. In the sky, half a moon was struggling against the glow in the west. Huge shadows came down from steep rocky slopes. Water was rushing. The woman was conscious only of her fatigue, her unspeakable fatigue, and the cold wind from the heights. She was not aware how moonlight replaced daylight. It happened while she travelled unconscious with weariness.

For some hours they travelled by moonlight. Then suddenly they came to a standstill. The men conversed in low tones for a moment.

'We camp here,' said the young man.

She waited for him to help her down. He merely stood holding the horse's bridle. She almost fell from the saddle, so fatigued.

They had chosen a place at the foot of rocks that still gave off a little warmth of the sun. One man cut pine-boughs, another erected little screens of pine-boughs against the rock for shelter, and put boughs of balsam pine for beds. The third made a small fire, to heat tortillas. They worked in silence.

The woman drank water. She did not want to eat – only to lie down.

'Where do I sleep?' she asked.

The young man pointed to one of the shelters. She crept in and lay inert. She did not care what happened to her, she was so weary, and so beyond everything. Through the twigs of spruce she could see the three men squatting round the fire on their hams, chewing the tortillas they picked from the ashes with their dark fingers, and drinking water from a gourd. They talked in low, muttering tones, with long intervals of silence. Her saddle and saddle-bags lay not far from the fire, unopened, untouched. The men were not interested in her or her belongings. There they squatted with their hats on their heads, eating, eating mechanically, like animals, the dark sarape with its fringe falling to the ground before and behind, the powerful dark legs naked and squatting like an animal's showing the dirty white shirt and the sort of loincloth which was the only other garment, underneath. And they showed no more sign of interest in her than if she had been a piece of venison they were bringing home from the hunt, and had hung inside a shelter.

After a while they carefully extinguished the fire, and went inside their own shelter. Watching through the screen of boughs, she had a moment's thrill of fear and anxiety, seeing the dark forms cross and pass silently in the moonlight. Would they attack her now?

But, no! They were as if oblivious of her. Her horse was hobbled; she could hear it hopping wearily. All was silent, mountain-silent, cold, deathly. She slept and woke and slept in a semi-conscious numbness of cold and fatigue. A long, long night, icy and eternal, and she aware that she had died.

Yet when there was a stirring, and a clink of flint and steel, and the form of a man crouching like a dog over a bone, at a red splutter of fire, and she knew it was morning coming, it seemed to her the night had passed too soon.

When the fire was going, she came out of her shelter with one real desire left: for coffee. The men were warming more tortillas.

'Can we make coffee?' she asked.

The young man looked at her, and she imagined the same faint spark of derision in his eyes. He shook his head.

'We don't take it,' he said. 'There is no time.'

And the elder men, squatting on their haunches, looked up at her in the terrible paling dawn, and there was not even derision in their eyes. Only that intense, yet remote, inhuman glitter which was terrible to her. They were inaccessible. They could not see her as a woman at all. As if she *were* not a woman. As if, perhaps, her whiteness took away all her womanhood, and left her as some giant, female white ant. That was all they could see in her.

Before the sun was up, she was in the saddle again, and they were climbing steeply, in the icy air. The sun came, and soon she was very hot, exposed to the glare in the bare places. It seemed to her they were climbing to the roof of the world. Beyond against heaven were slashes of snow.

During the course of the morning, they came to a place where the horse could not go farther. They rested for a time with a great slant of living rock in front of them, like the glossy breast of some earth-beast. Across this rock, along a wavering crack, they had to go. It seemed to her that for hours she went in torment, on her hands and knees, from crack to crevice, along the slanting face of this pure rock-mountain. An Indian in front and an Indian behind walked slowly erect, shod with sandals of braided leather. But she in her riding-boots dared not stand erect.

Yet what she wondered, all the time, was why she persisted in clinging and crawling along these mile-long sheets of rock. Why she did not hurl herself down, and have done? The world was below her.

When they emerged at last on a stony slope, she looked back, and saw the third Indian coming carrying her saddle and saddle-bags on his back, the whole hung from a band across his forehead. And he had his hat in his hand, as he stepped slowly, with the slow, soft, heavy tread of the Indian, unwavering in the chinks of rock, as if along a scratch in the mountain's iron shield.

The stony slope led downwards. The Indians seemed to grow excited. One ran ahead at a slow trot, disappearing round the curve of stones. And the track curved round and down, till at last in the full blaze of the mid-morning sun, they could see a valley below them, between walls of rock, as in a great wide chasm let in the mountains. A green valley, with a river, and trees, and clusters of low flat sparkling houses. It was all tiny and perfect, three thousand feet below. Even the flat bridge over the stream, and the square with the houses around it, the bigger buildings piled up at opposite ends of the square, the tall cottonwood trees, the pastures and stretches of yellow-sere maize, the patches of brown sheep or goats in the distance, on the slopes, the railed enclosures by the stream-side. There it was, all small and perfect, looking magical, as any place will look magical, seen from the mountains above. The usual thing was that the low houses glittered white, white-washed, looking like crystals of salt, or silver. This frightened her.

They began the long, winding descent at the head of the barranca, following the stream that rushed and fell. At first it was all rocks: then the pine trees began, and soon, the silver-limbed aspens. The flowers of autumn, big pink daisy-like flowers, and white ones, and many yellow flowers, were in profusion. But she had to sit down and rest, she was so weary. And she saw the bright flowers shadowily, as pale shadows hovering, as one who is dead must see them.

At length came grass and pasture-slopes between mingled aspen and pine trees. A shepherd, naked in the sun save for his hat and his cotton loincloth, was driving his brown sheep away. In a grove of trees they sat and waited, she and the young Indian. The one with the saddle had also gone forward.

They heard a sound of someone coming. It was three men, in fine sarapes of red and orange and yellow and black, and with brilliant feather head-dresses. The oldest had his grey hair braided with fur, and his red and orange-yellow sarape was covered with curious black markings, like a leopard-skin. The other two were not grey-haired, but they were elders too. Their blankets were in stripes, and their headdresses not so elaborate.

The young Indian addressed the elders in a few quiet words. They listened without answering or looking at him or at the woman, keeping their faces averted and their eyes turned to the ground, only listening. And at length they turned and looked at the woman.

The old chief, or medicine-man, whatever he was, had a deeply wrinkled and lined face of dark bronze, with a few sparse grey hairs round the mouth. Two long braids of grey hair, braided with fur and coloured feathers, hung on his shoulders. And yet, it was only his eyes that mattered. They were black and of extraordinary piercing strength, without a qualm of misgivings in their demonish, dauntless power. He looked into the eyes of the white woman with a long, piercing look, seeking she knew not what. She summoned all her strength to meet his eyes and keep up her guard. But it was no good. He was not looking at her as one human being looks at another. He never even perceived her resistance or her challenge, but looked past them both, into she knew not what.

She could see it was hopeless to expect any human communication with this old being.

He turned and said a few words to the young Indian.

'He asks what do you seek here?' said the young man in Spanish.

'I? Nothing! I only came to see what it was like.'

This was again translated, and the old man turned his eyes on her once more. Then he spoke again, in his low muttering tone, to the young Indian.

'He says, why does she leave her house with the white men? Does she want to bring the white man's God to the Chilchui?'

'No,' she replied, foolhardy. 'I came away from the white man's God myself. I came to look for the God of the Chilchui.'

Profound silence followed, when this was translated. Then the old man spoke again, in a small voice almost of weariness.

'Does the white woman seek the gods of the Chilchui because she is weary of her own God?' came the question.

'Yes, she does. She is tired of the white man's God,' she replied, thinking that was what they wanted her to say. She would like to serve the gods of the Chilchui.

She was aware of an extraordinary thrill of triumph and exultance passing through the Indians, in the tense silence that followed when this was translated. Then they all looked at her with piercing black eyes, in which a steely covetous intent glittered in-comprehensible. She was the more puzzled, as there was nothing sensual or sexual in the look. It had a terrible glittering purity that was beyond her. She was afraid, she would have been paralysed with fear, had not some-thing died within her, leaving her with a cold, watchful wonder only.

The elders talked a little while, then the two went away, leaving her with the young man and the oldest chief. The old man now looked at her with a certain solicitude.

'He says you are tired?' asked the young man.

'Very tired,' she said.

'The men will bring you a carriage,' said the young Indian.

The carriage, when it came, proved to be a litter consisting of a sort of hammock of dark woollen frieze, slung on to a pole which was borne on the shoulders of two long-haired Indians. The woollen hammock was spread on the ground, she sat down on it, and the two men raised the pole to their shoulders. Swinging rather as if she were a sack, she was carried out of the grove of trees, following the old chief, whose leopard-spotted blanket moved curiously in the sunlight.

They had emerged in the valley-head. Just in front were the maize fields, with ripe ears of maize. The corn was not very tall, in this high altitude. The well-worn path went between it, and all she could see was the erect form of the old chief, in the flame and black sarape, stepping soft and heavy and swift, his head forward, looking neither to right nor to left. Her bearers followed, stepping rhythmically, the long blue-black hair glistening like a river down the naked shoulders of the man in front.

They passed the maize, and came to a big wall or earth-work made of earth and adobe bricks. The wooden doors were open. Passing on, they were in a network of small gardens, full of flowers and herbs and fruit trees, each garden watered by a tiny ditch of running water. Among each cluster of trees and flowers was a small, glittering white house, windowless, and with closed door. The place was a network of little paths, small streams, and little bridges among square, flowering gardens.

Following the broadest path – a soft narrow track between leaves and grass, a path worn smooth by centuries of human feet, no hoof of horse nor any wheel to disfigure it – they came to the little river of swift bright water, and crossed on a log bridge. Everything was silent – there was no human being anywhere. The road went on under magnificent cottonwood trees. It emerged suddenly outside the central plaza or square of the village.

This was a long oblong of low white houses with flat roofs, and two bigger buildings, having as it were little square huts piled on top of bigger long huts, stood at either end of the oblong, facing each other rather askew. Every little house was a dazzling white, save for the great round beam-ends which projected under the flat eaves, and for the flat roofs. Round each of the bigger buildings, on the outside of the square, was a stockyard fence, inside which was garden with trees and flowers, and various small houses.

Not a soul was in sight. They passed silently between the houses into the central square. This was quite bare and arid, the earth trodden smooth by endless generations of passing feet, passing across from door to door. All the doors of the windowless houses gave on to this blank square, but all the doors were closed. The firewood lay near the threshold, a clay oven was still smoking, but there was no sign of moving life.

The old man walked straight across the square to the big house at the end, where the two upper storeys, as in a house of toy bricks, stood each one smaller than the lower one. A stone staircase, outside, led up to the roof of the first storey.

At the foot of this staircase the litter-bearers stood still, and lowered the woman to the ground.

'You will come up,' said the young Indian who spoke Spanish.

She mounted the stone stairs to the earthen roof of the first house, which formed a platform round the wall of the second storey. She followed around this platform to the back of the big house. There they descended again, into the garden at the rear.

So far they had seen no one. But now two men appeared, bare-headed, with long braided hair, and wearing a sort of white shirt gathered into a loincloth. These went along with the three newcomers, across the garden where red flowers and yellow flowers were blooming, to a long, low white house. There they entered without knocking.

It was dark inside. There was a low murmur of men's voices. Several men were present, their white shirts showing in the gloom, their dark faces invisible. They were sitting on a great log of smooth old wood, that lay along the far wall. And save for this log, the room seemed empty. But no, in the dark at one end was a couch, a sort of bed, and someone lying there, covered with furs.

The old Indian in the spotted sarape, who had accompanied the woman, now took off his hat and his blanket and his sandals. Laying them aside, he approached the couch, and spoke in a low voice. For some moments there was no answer. Then an old man, with the snow-white hair hanging round his darkly-visible face, roused himself like a vision, and leaned on one elbow, looking vaguely at the company, in tense silence.

The grey-haired Indian spoke again, and then the young Indian, taking the woman's hand, led her forward. In her linen riding habit, and black boots and hat, and her pathetic bit of red tie, she stood there beside the fur-covered bed of the old, old man, who sat reared up, leaning on one elbow, remote as a ghost, his white hair streaming in disorder, his face almost black, yet with a far-off intentness, not of this world, leaning forward to look at her.

His face was so old, it was like dark glass, and the few curling hairs that sprang white from his lips and chin were quite incredible. The long white locks fell unbraided and disorderly on either side of the glassy dark face. And under a faint powder of white eyebrows, the black eyes of the old chief looked at her as if from the far, far dead, seeing something that was never to be seen.

At last he spoke a few deep, hollow words, as if to the dark air.

'He says, do you bring your heart to the god of the Chilchui?' translated the young Indian.

'Tell him yes,' she said, automatically.

There was a pause. The old Indian spoke again, as if to the air. One of the men present went out. There was a silence as if of eternity, in the dim room that was lighted only through the open door.

The woman looked round. Four old men with grey hair sat on the log by the wall facing the door. Two other men, powerful and impassive, stood near the door. They all had long hair, and wore white shirts gathered into a loincloth. Their powerful legs were naked and dark. There was a silence like eternity.

At length the man returned, with white and dark clothing on his arm. The young Indian took them, and holding them in front of the woman, said:

'You must take off your clothes, and put these on.'

'If all you men will go out,' she said.

'No one will hurt you,' he said quietly.

'Not while you men are here,' she said.

He looked at the two men by the door. They came quickly forward, and suddenly gripped her arms as she stood, without hurting her, but with great power. Then two of the old men came, and with curious skill slit her boots down with keen knives, and drew them off, and slit her clothing so that it came away from her. In a few moments she stood there white and uncovered. The old man on the bed spoke, and they turned her round for him to see. He spoke again, and the young Indian deftly took the pins and comb from her fair hair, so that it fell over her shoulders in a bunchy tangle.

Then the old man spoke again. The Indian led her to the bedside. The white-haired, glassy-dark old man moistened his fingertips at his mouth, and most delicately touched her on the breasts and on the body, then on the back. And she winced strangely each time, as the fingertips drew along her skin, as if Death itself were touching her.

And she wondered, almost sadly, why she did not feel shamed in her nakedness. She only felt sad and lost. Because nobody felt ashamed. The elder men were all dark and tense with some other deep, gloomy, incomprehensible emotion, which suspended all her agitation while the young Indian had a strange look of ecstasy on his face. And she, she was only utterly strange and beyond herself, as if her body were not her own.

They gave her the new clothing: a long white cotton shift, that came to her knees: then a tunic of thick blue woollen stuff, embroidered with scarlet and green flowers. It was fastened over one shoulder only, and belted with a braid sash of scarlet and black wool.

When she was thus dressed, they took her away, barefoot, to a little house in the stockaded garden. The young Indian told her she might have what she wanted. She asked for water to wash herself. He brought it in a jar, together with a long wooden bowl. Then he fastened the gate-door of her house, and left her a prisoner. She could see through the bars of the great-door of her house, the red flowers of the garden, and a humming bird. Then from the roof of the big house she heard the long, heavy sound of a drum, unearthly to her in its summons, and an uplifting voice calling from the house-top in a strange language, with a far-away emotionless intonation, delivering some speech or message. And she listened as if from the dead.

But she was very tired. She lay down on a couch of skins, pulling over her the blanket of dark wool, and she slept, giving up everything.

When she woke it was late afternoon, and the young Indian was entering with a basket-tray containing food, tortillas and corn-mush with bits of meat, probably mutton, and a drink made of honey, and some fresh plums. He brought her also a long garland of red and yellow flowers with knots of blue buds at the end. He sprinkled the garland with water from a jar, then offered it to her, with a smile. He seemed very gentle and thoughtful, and on his face and in his dark eyes was a curious look of triumph and ecstasy, that frightened her a little. The glitter had gone from the black eyes, with their curving dark lashes, and he would look at her with this strange soft glow of ecstasy that was not quite human, and terribly impersonal, and which made her uneasy.

'Is there anything you want?' he said, in his low, slow, melodious voice, that always seemed withheld, as if he were speaking aside to somebody else, or as if he did not want to let the sound come out to her.

'Am I going to be kept a prisoner here?' she asked.

'No, you can walk in the garden tomorrow,' he said softly. Always this curious solicitude.

'Do you like that drink?' he said, offering her a little earthenware cup. 'It is very refreshing.'

She sipped the liquor curiously. It was made with herbs and sweetened with honey, and had a strange, lingering flavour. The young man watched her with gratification.

'It has a peculiar taste,' she said.

'It is very refreshing,' he replied, his black eyes resting on her always with that look of gratified ecstasy. Then he went away. And presently she began to be sick, and to vomit violently, as if she had no control over herself.

Afterwards she felt a great soothing languor steal over her, her limbs felt strong and loose and full of languor, and she lay on her couch listening to the sounds of the village, watching the yellowing sky, smelling the scent of burning cedar-wood, or pine-wood. So distinctly she heard the yapping of tiny dogs, the shuffle of far-off feet, the murmur of voices, so keenly she detected the smell of smoke, and flowers, and evening falling, so vividly she saw the one bright star infinitely remote, stirring above the sunset, that she felt as if all her senses were diffused on the air, that she could distinguish the sound of evening flowers unfolding, and the actual crystal sound of the heavens, as the vast belts of the world-atmosphere slid past one another, and as if the moisture ascending and the moisture descending in the air resounded like some harp in the cosmos.

She was a prisoner in her house and in the stockaded garden, but she scarcely minded. And it was days before she realized that she never saw another woman. Only the men, the elderly men of the big house, that she imagined must be some sort of temple, and the men priests of some sort. For they always had the same colours, red, orange, yellow, and black, and the same grave, abstracted demeanour.

Sometimes an old man would come and sit in her room with her, in absolute silence. None spoke any language but Indian, save the one younger man. The older men would smile at her, and sit with her for an hour at a time, sometimes smiling at her when she spoke in Spanish, but never answering save with this slow, benevolent-seeming smile. And they gave off a feeling of almost fatherly solicitude. Yet their dark eyes, brooding over her, had something away in their depths that was awesomely ferocious and relentless. They would cover it with a smile, at once, if they felt her looking. But she had seen it.

Always they treated her with this curious impersonal solicitude, this utterly impersonal gentleness, as an old man treats a child. But underneath it she felt there was something else, something terrible. When her old visitor had gone away, in his silent, insidious, fatherly fashion, a shock of fear would come over her; though of what she knew not.

The young Indian would sit and talk with her freely, as if with great candour. But with him, too, she felt that everything real was unsaid. Perhaps it was unspeakable. His big dark eyes would rest on her almost cherishingly, touched with ecstasy, and his beautiful, slow, languorous voice would trail out its simple, ungrammatical Spanish. He told her he was the grandson of the old, old man, son of the man in the spotted sarape: and they were caciques, kings from the old, old days, before even the Spaniards came. But he himself had been in Mexico City, and also in the United States. He had worked as a labourer, building the roads in Los Angeles. He had travelled as far as Chicago.

'Don't you speak English, then?' she asked.

His eyes rested on her with a curious look of duplicity and conflict, and he mutely shook his head.

'What did you do with your long hair, when you were in the United States?' she asked. 'Did you cut it off?'

Again, with the look of torment in his eyes, he shook his head.

'No,' he said, in a low, subdued voice, 'I wore a hat, and a handkerchief tied around my head.'

And he relapsed into silence, as if of tormented memories.

'Are you the only man of your people who has been to the United States?' she asked him.

'Yes. I am the only one who has been away from here for a long time. The others come back soon, in one week. They don't stay away. The old men don't let them.'

'And why did you go?'

'The old men want me to go – because I shall be the Cacique–'

He talked always with the same naïveté, an almost childish candour. But she felt that this was perhaps just the effect of his Spanish. Or perhaps speech altogether was unreal to him. Anyhow, she felt that all the real things were kept back.

He came and sat with her a good deal – sometimes more than she wished – as if he wanted to be near her. She asked him if he was married. He said he was – with two children.

'I should like to see your children,' she said.

But he answered only with that smile, a sweet, almost ecstatic smile, above which the dark eyes hardly changed from their enigmatic abstraction.

It was curious, he would sit with her by the hour, without ever making her self-conscious, or sex-conscious. He seemed to have no sex, as he sat there so still and gentle and apparently sub-missive, with his head bent a little forward, and the river of glistening black hair streaming mai-denly over his shoulders.

Yet when she looked again, she saw his shoulders broad and powerful, his eyebrows black and level, the short, curved, obstinate black lashes over his lowered eyes, the small, fur-like line of moustache above his blackish, heavy lips, and the strong chin, and she knew that in some other mysterious way he was darkly and powerfully male. And he, feeling her watching him, would glance up at her swiftly with a dark, lurking look in his eyes, which immediately he veiled with that half-sad smile.

The days and the weeks went by, in a vague kind of contentment. She was uneasy sometimes, feeling she had lost the power over herself. She was not in her own power, she was under the spell of some other control. And at times she had moments of terror and horror. But then these Indians would come and sit with her, casting their insidious spell over her by their very silent presence, their silent, sexless, powerful physical presence. As they sat they seemed to take her will away, leaving her will-less and victim of her own indifference. And the young man would bring her sweetened drink, often the same emetic drink, but sometimes other kinds. And after drinking, the languor filled her heavy limbs, her senses seemed to float in the air, listening, hearing. They had brought her a little female dog, which she called Flora. And once, in the trance of her senses, she felt she *heard* the little dog conceive, in her tiny womb, and begin to be complex, with young. And another day she could hear the vast sound of the earth going round, like some immense arrow-string booming.

But as the days grew shorter and colder, when she was cold, she would get a sudden revival of her will, and a desire to go out, to go away. And she insisted to the young man, she wanted to go out.

So one day, they let her climb to the topmost roof of the big house where she was, and look down the square. It was the day of the big dance, but not everybody was dancing. Women with babies in their arms stood in their doorways, watching. Opposite, at the other end of the square, there was a throng before the other big house, and a small, brilliant group on the terrace-roof of the first storey, in front of the wide-open doors of the upper storey. Through these wide-open doors she could see fire glinting in darkness and priests in headdresses of black and yellow and scarlet feathers, wearing robe-like blankets of black and red and yellow, with long green fringe, were moving about. A big drum was beating slowly and regularly, in the dense, Indian silence. The crowd below waited –

Then a drum started on a high beat, and there came the deep, powerful burst of men singing a heavy, savage music, like a wind roaring in some timeless forest, many mature men singing in one breath, like the wind; and long lines of dancers walked out from under the big house. Men with naked, golden-bronze bodies and streaming black hair, tufts of red and yellow feathers on their arms, and kilts of white frieze with a bar of heavy red and black and green embroidery round their waists, bending slightly forward and stamping the earth in their absorbed, monotonous stamp of the dance, a fox-fur, hung by the nose from their belt behind, swaying with the sumptuous swaying of a beautiful fox-fur, the tip of the tail

writhing above the dancer's heels. And after each
man, a woman with a strange elaborate headdress
of feathers and seashells, and wearing a short black
tunic, moving erect, holding up tufts of feathers in
each hand, swaying her wrists rhythmically and
subtly beating the earth with her bare feet.

So, the long line of the dance unfurling from
the big house opposite. And from the big house
beneath her, strange scent of incense, strange
tense silence, then the answering bursts of inhuman male singing, and the long line of the dance
unfurling.

It went on all day, the insistence of the drum,
the cavernous, roaring, storm-like sound of male
singing, the incessant swinging of the fox-skins
behind the powerful, gold-bronze stamping legs
of the men, the autumn sun from a perfect blue
heaven pouring on the rivers of black hair, men's
and women's, the valley all still, the walls of rock
beyond, the awful huge bulking of the mountain
against the pure sky, its snow seething with sheer
whiteness.

For hours and hours she watched, spellbound,
and as if drugged. And in all the terrible persis-
tence of the drumming and the primeval, rushing
deep singing, and the endless stamping of the
dance of fox-tailed men, the tread of heavy, bird-
erect women in their black tunics, she seemed at
last to feel her own death; her own obliteration.
As if she were to be obliterated from the field of
life again. In the strange towering symbols on the
heads of the changeless, absorbed women she

seemed to read once more the *Mene Mene Tekel Upharsin*. Her kind of womanhood, intensely personal and individual, was to be obliterated again, and the great primeval symbols were to tower once more over the fallen individual independence of woman. The sharpness and the quivering nervous consciousness of the highly-bred white woman was to be destroyed again, womanhood was to be cast once more into the great stream of impersonal sex and impersonal passion. Strangely, as if clairvoyant, she saw the immense sacrifice prepared. And she went back to her little house in a trance of agony.

After this, there was always a certain agony when she heard the drums at evening, and the strange uplifted savage sound of men singing round the drum, like wild creatures howling to the invisible gods of the moon and the vanished sun. Something of the chuckling, sobbing cry of the coyote, something of the exultant bark of the fox, the far-off wild melancholy exultance of the howling wolf, the torment of the puma's scream, and the insistence of the ancient fierce human male, with his lapses of tenderness and his abiding ferocity.

Sometimes she would climb the high roof after nightfall, and listen to the dim cluster of young men round the drum on the bridge just beyond the square, singing by the hour. Sometimes there would be a fire, and in the fire-glow, men in their white shirts or naked save for a loincloth, would be dancing and stamping like spectres, hour after hour in the dark cold air, within the fire-glow, for ever dancing and stamping like turkeys, or dropping squatting by the fire to rest throwing their blankets round them.

'Why do you all have the same colours?' she asked the young Indian. 'Why do you all have red and yellow and black, over your white shirts? And the women have black tunics?'

He looked into her eyes, curiously, and the faint, evasive smile came on to his face. Behind the smile lay a soft, strange malignancy.

'Because our men are the fire and the daytime, and our women are the spaces between the stars at night,' he said.

'Aren't the women even stars?' she said.

'No. We say they are the spaces between the stars, that keep the stars apart.'

He looked at her oddly, and again the touch of derision came into his eyes.

'White people,' he said, 'they know nothing. They are like children, always with toys. We know the sun, and we know the moon. And we say, when a white woman sacrifice herself to our gods, then our gods will begin to make the world again, and the white man's gods will fall to pieces.'

'How sacrifice herself?' she asked quickly.

And he, as quickly covered, covered himself with a subtle smile.

'She sacrifice her own gods and come to our gods, I mean that,' he said, soothingly.

But she was not reassured. An icy pang of fear and certainty was at her heart.

'The sun he is alive at one end of the sky,' he continued, 'and the moon lives at the other end. And the man all the time have to keep the sun happy in his side of the sky, and the woman have to keep the moon quiet at her side of the sky. All the time she have to work at this. And the sun can't ever go into the house of the moon, and the moon can't ever go into the house of the sun, in the sky. So woman, she asks the moon to come into her cave, inside her. And the man, he draws the sun down till he has the power of the sun. All the time he do this. Then when the man gets a woman, the sun goes into the cave of the moon, and that is how everything in the world starts.'

She listened, watching him closely, as one enemy watches another who is speaking with double meaning.

'Then,' she said, 'why aren't you Indians masters of the white men?'

'Because,' he said, 'the Indian got weak, and lost his power with the sun, so the white men stole the sun. But they can't keep him – they don't know how. They got him, but they don't know what to do with him, like a boy who catch a big grizzly bear, and can't kill him, and can't run away from him. The grizzly bear eats the boy that catch him, when he want to run away from him. White men don't know what they are doing with the sun, and white women don't know what they do with the moon. The moon she got angry with white women, like a puma when someone kills her little ones. The moon, she bites white women

– here inside,' and he pressed his side. 'The moon, she is angry in a white woman's cave. The Indian can see it – and soon,' he added, 'the Indian women get the moon back and keep her quiet in their house. And the Indian men get the sun, and the power over all the world. White men don't know what the sun is. They never know.'

He subsided into a curious exultant silence.

'But,' she faltered, 'why do you hate us so? Why do you hate me?'

He looked up suddenly with a light on his face, and a startling flame of a smile.

'No, we don't hate,' he said softly, looking with a curious glitter into her face.

'You do,' she said, forlorn and hopeless.

And after a moment's silence, he rose and went away.

Winter had now come, in the high valley, with snow that melted in the day's sun, and nights that were bitter cold. She lived on, in a kind of daze, feeling her power ebbing more and more away from her, as if her will were leaving her. She felt always in the same relaxed, confused, victimized state, unless the sweetened herb drink would numb her mind altogether, and release her senses into a sort of heightened, mystic acuteness and a feeling as if she were diffusing out deliciously into the harmony of things. This at length became the only state of consciousness she really recognized: this exquisite sense of bleeding out into the higher beauty and harmony of things. Then she could actually hear the great stars in heaven, which she saw through her door, speaking from their motion and brightness, saying things perfectly to the cosmos, as they trod in perfect ripples, like bells on the floor of heaven, passing one another and grouping in the timeless dance, with the spaces of dark between. And she could hear the snow on a cold, cloudy day twittering and faintly whistling in the sky, like birds that flock and fly away in autumn, suddenly calling farewell to the invisible moon, and slipping out of the plains of the air, releasing peaceful warmth. She herself would call to the arrested snow to fall from the upper air. She would call to the unseen moon to cease to be angry, to make peace again with the unseen sun like a woman who ceases to be angry in her house. And she would smell the sweetness of the moon relaxing to the sun in the wintry heaven, when the snow fell in a faint, cold-perfumed relaxation, as the peace of the sun mingled again in a sort of unison with the peace of the moon.

She was aware, too, of the sort of shadow that was on the Indians of the valley, a deep, stoical disconsolation, almost religious in its depth.

'We have lost our power over the sun, and we are trying to get him back. But he is wild with us, and shy like a horse that has got away. We have to go through a lot.' So the young Indian said to her, looking into her eyes with a strained meaning. And she, as if bewitched, replied:

'I hope you will get him back.'

The smile of triumph flew over his face.

'Do you hope it?' he said.

'I do,' she answered fatally.

'Then all right,' he said. 'We shall get him.'

And he went away in exultance.

She felt she was drifting on some consummation, which she had no will to avoid, yet which seemed heavy and finally terrible to her.

It must have been almost December, for the days were short, when she was taken again before the aged man, and stripped of her clothing, and touched with the old fingertips.

The aged cacique looked her in the eyes, with his eyes of lonely, far-off, black intentness, and murmured something to her.

'He wants you to make the sign of peace,' the young man translated, showing her the gesture. 'Peace and farewell to him.'

She was fascinated by the black, glass-like, intent eyes of the old cacique, that watched her without blinking, like a basilisk's, overpowering her. In their depths also she saw a certain fatherly compassion, and pleading. She put her hand before her face, in the required manner, making the sign of peace and farewell. He made the sign of peace back again to her, then sank among his furs. She thought he was going to die, and that he knew it.

There followed a day of ceremonial, when she was brought out before all the people, in a blue blanket with white fringe, and holding blue feathers in her hands. Before an altar of one house, she was perfumed with incense and sprinkled with ash. Below the altar of the oppo-

site house she was fumigated again with incense
by the gorgeous, terrifying priests in yellow and
scarlet and black, their faces painted with scarlet
paint. And then they threw water on her. Meanwhile she was faintly aware of the fire on the altar,
the heavy, heavy sound of a drum, the heavy
sound of men beginning powerfully, deeply,
savagely to sing, the swaying of the crowd of
faces in the plaza below, and the formation for a
sacred dance.

But at this time her commonplace consciousness was numb, she was aware of her immediate
surroundings as shadows, almost immaterial. With
refined and heightened senses she could hear the
sound of the earth winging on its journey, like a
shot arrow, the ripple-rustling of the air, and the
boom of the great arrow-string. And it seemed to
her there were two great influences in the upper
air, one golden towards the sun, and one invisible
silver; the first travelling like rain ascending to the
gold presence sunwards, the second like rain
silverily descending the ladders of space towards
the hovering, lurking clouds over the snowy
mountain-top. Then between them, another
presence, waiting to shake himself free of moisture, of heavy white snow that had mysteriously
collected about him. And in summer, like a
scorched eagle, he would wait to shake himself
clear of the weight of heavy sunbeams. And he
was coloured like fire. And he was always shaking
himself clear, of snow or of heavy heat, like an
eagle rustling.

Then there was a still stranger presence, standing watching from the blue distance, always watching. Sometimes running in upon the wind, or shimmering in the heat-waves. The blue wind itself, rushing as it were out of the holes in the earth into the sky, rushing out of the sky down upon the earth. The blue wind, the go-between, the invisible ghost that belonged to two worlds, that played upon the ascending and the descending chords of the rains.

More and more her ordinary personal consciousness had left her, she had gone into that other state of passional cosmic consciousness, like one who is drugged. The Indians, with their heavily religious natures, had made her succumb to their vision.

Only one personal question she asked the young Indian:

'Why am I the only one that wears blue?'

'It is the colour of the wind. It is the colour of what goes away and is never coming back, but which is always here, waiting like death among us. It is the colour of the dead. And it is the colour that stands away off, looking at us from the distance, that cannot come near to us. When we go near, it goes farther. It can't be near. We are all brown and yellow and black hair, and white teeth and red blood. We are the ones that are here. You with blue eyes, you are the messengers from the far-away, you cannot stay, and now it is time for you to go back.'

'Where to?' she asked.

'To the way-off things like the sun and the blue mother of rain, and tell them that we are the people on the world again, and we can bring the sun to the moon again, like a red horse to a blue mare; we are the people. The white women have driven back the moon in the sky, won't let her come to the sun. So the sun is angry. And the Indian must give the moon to the sun.'

'How?' she said.

'The white woman got to die and go like the wind to the sun, tell him the Indians will open the gate to him. And the Indian women will open the gate to the moon. The white women don't let the moon come down out of the blue corral. The moon used to come down among the Indian women, like a white goat among the flowers. And the sun want to come down to the Indian men, like an eagle to the pine trees. The sun he is shut out behind the white man, and the moon she is shut out behind the white woman, and they can't get away. They are angry, everything in the world gets angrier. The Indian says, he will give the white woman to the sun, so the sun will leap over the white man and come to the Indian again. And the moon will be surprised, she will see the gate open, and she not know which way to go. But the Indian woman will call to the moon, *Come! Come! Come back into my grasslands. The wicked white woman can't harm you any more.* Then the sun will look over the heads of the white men, and see the moon in the pastures of our women, with the Red Men standing around like pine trees. Then he will leap over the heads of the white men, and come running past to the Indians through the spruce trees. And we, who are red and black and yellow, we who stay, we shall have the sun on our right hand and the moon on our left. So we can bring the rain down out of the blue meadows, and up out of the black; and we can call the wind that tells the corn to grow, when we ask him, and we shall make the clouds to break, and the sheep to have twin lambs. And we shall be full of power, like a spring day. But the white people will be a hard winter, without snow –'

'But,' said the white woman, 'I don't shut out the moon – how can I?'

'Yes,' he said, 'you shut the gate, and then laugh, think you have it all your own way.'

She could never quite understand the way he looked at her. He was always so curiously gentle, and his smile was so soft. Yet there was such a glitter in his eyes, and an unrelenting sort of hate came out of his words, a strange, profound, impersonal hate. Personally he liked her, she was sure. He was gentle with her, attracted by her in some strange, soft, passionless way. But impersonally he hated her with a mystic hatred. He would smile at her, winningly. Yet if, the next moment, she glanced round at him unawares, she would catch that gleam of pure after-hate in his eyes.

'Have I got to die and be given to the sun?' she asked.

'Sometime,' he said, laughing evasively. 'Sometime we all die.'

They were gentle with her, and very considerate with her. Strange men, the old priests and the young cacique alike, they watched over her and cared for her like women. In their soft, insidious understanding, there was something womanly. Yet their eyes, with that strange glitter, and their dark, shut mouths that would open to the broad jaw, the small, strong, white teeth, had something very primitively male and cruel.

One wintry day when snow was falling, they took her to a great dark chamber in the big house. The fire was burning in a corner on a high raised dais under a sort of hood or canopy of adobe-work. She saw in the fire-glow, the glowing bodies of the almost naked priests, and strange symbols on the roof and walls of the chamber. There was no door or window in the chamber, they had descended by a ladder from the roof. And the fire of pinewood danced continually, showing walls painted with strange devices, which she could not understand, and a ceiling of poles making a curious pattern of black and red and yellow, and alcoves or niches in which were curious objects she could not discern.

The older priests were going through some ceremony near the fire, in silence, intense Indian silence. She was seated on a low projection of the wall, opposite the fire, two men seated beside her. Presently they gave her a drink from a cup, which

she took gladly, because of the semi-trance it
would induce.

In the darkness and in the silence she was
accurately aware of everything that happened to
her: how they took off her clothes, and standing
before a great, weird device on the wall, coloured
blue and white and black, washed her all over
with water and the amole infusion; washed even
her hair, softly, carefully, and dried it on white
cloths, till it was soft and glistening. Then they laid
her on a couch under another great indecipher-
able image of red and black and yellow, and now
rubbed all her body with sweet-scented oil, and
massaged all her limbs, and her back, and her
sides, with a long, strange, hypnotic massage.
Their dark hands were incredibly powerful, yet
soft with a watery softness she could not understand. And the dark faces, leaning near her white
body, she saw were darkened with red pigment,
with lines of yellow round the cheeks. And the
dark eyes glittered absorbed, as the hands worked
upon the soft white body of the woman.

They were so impersonal, absorbed in something that was beyond her. They never saw her as
a personal woman: she could tell that. She was
some mystic object to them, some vehicle of
passions too remote for her to grasp. Herself in a
state of trance, she watched their faces bending
over her, dark, strangely glistening with the
transparent red paint, and lined with bars of
yellow. And in this weird, luminous-dark mask
of living face, the eyes were fixed with an

unchanging steadfast gleam, and the purplish-pigmented lips were closed in a full, sinister, sad grimness. The immense fundamental sadness, the grimness of ultimate decision, the fixity of revenge, and the nascent exultance of those that are going to triumph – these things she could read in their faces, as she lay and was rubbed into a misty glow, by their uncanny dark hands. Her limbs, her flesh, her very bones at last seemed to be diffusing into a roseate sort of mist, in which her consciousness hovered like some sun-gleam in a flushed cloud.

She knew the gleam would fade, the cloud would go grey. But at present she did not believe it. She knew she was a victim; that all this elaborate work upon her was the work of victimizing her. But she did not mind. She wanted it.

Later, they put a short blue tunic on her and took her to the upper terrace, and presented her to the people. She saw the plaza below her full of dark faces and of glittering eyes. There was no pity: only the curious hard exultance. The people gave a subdued cry when they saw her, and she shuddered. But she hardly cared.

Next day was the last. She slept in a chamber of the big house. At dawn they put on her a big blue blanket with a fringe, and led her out into the plaza, among the throng of silent, dark-blanketed people. There was pure white snow on the ground, and the dark people in their dark-brown blankets looked like inhabitants of another world.

A large drum was slowly pounding, and an old priest was declaiming from a housetop. But it was not till noon that a litter came forth, and the people gave that low, animal cry which was so moving. In the sack-like litter sat the old, old cacique, his white hair braided with black braid and large turquoise stones. His face was like a piece of obsidian. He lifted his hand in token, and the litter stopped in front of her. Fixing her with his old eyes, he spoke to her for a few moments, in his hollow voice. No one translated.

Another litter came, and she was placed in it. Four priests moved ahead, in their scarlet and yellow and black, with plumed headdresses. Then came the litter of the old cacique. Then the light drums began, and two groups of singers burst simultaneously into song, male and wild. And the golden-red, almost naked men, adorned with ceremonial feathers and kilts, the rivers of black hair down their backs, formed into two files and began to tread the dance. So they threaded out of the snowy plaza, in two long, sumptuous lines of dark red-gold and black and fur, swaying with a faint tinkle of bits of shell and flint, winding over the snow between the two bee-clusters of men who sang around the drum.

Slowly they moved out, and her litter, with its attendance of feathered, lurid, dancing priests, moved after. Everybody danced the tread of the dance-step, even, subtly, the litter-bearers. And out of the plaza they went, past smoking ovens, on the trail to the great cottonwood trees, that stood like grey-silver lace against the blue sky, bare and exquisite above the snow. The river, diminished, rushed among fangs of ice. The chequer-squares of gardens with fences were all snowy, and the white houses now looked yellowish.

The whole valley glittered intolerably with pure snow, away to the walls of the standing rock. And across the flat cradle of snow-bed wound the long thread of the dance, shaking slowly and sumptuously in its orange and black motion. The high drums thudded quickly, and on the crystalline frozen air the swell and roar of the chant of savages was like an obsession.

She sat looking out of her litter with big, transfixed blue eyes, under which were the wan markings of her drugged weariness. She knew she was going to die, among the glisten of this snow, at the hands of this savage, sumptuous people. And as she stared at the blaze of blue sky above the slashed and ponderous mountain, she thought: 'I am dead already. What difference does it make, the transition from the dead I am to the dead I shall be, very soon!' Yet her soul sickened and felt wan.

The strange procession trailed on, in perpetual dance, slowly across the plain of snow, and then entered the slopes between the pine trees. She saw the copper-dark men dancing the dance-tread, onwards, between the copper-pale tree trunks. And at last she, too, in her swaying litter, entered the pine trees.

They were travelling on and on, upwards, across the snow under the trees, past the superb shafts of pale, flaked copper, the rustle and shake and tread of the threading dance, penetrating into the forest, into the mountain. They were following a stream-bed: but the stream was dry, like summer, dried up by the frozenness of the headwaters. There were dark, red-bronze willow bushes with wattles like wild hair, and pallid aspen trees looking like cold flesh against the snow. Then jutting dark rocks.

At last she could tell that the dancers were moving forward no more. Nearer and nearer she came upon the drums, as to a lair of mysterious animals. Then through the bushes she emerged into a strange amphitheatre. Facing was a great wall of hollow rock, down the front of which hung a great, dripping, fang-like spoke of ice. The ice came pouring over the rock from the precipice above, and then stood arrested, dripping out of high heaven, almost down to the hollow stones where the stream-pool should be below. But the pool was dry.

On either side of the dry pool, the lines of dancers had formed, and the dance was continuing without intermission, against a background of bushes.

But what she felt was that fanged inverted pinnacle of ice, hanging from the lip of the dark precipice above. And behind the great rope of ice, she saw the leopard-like figures of priests climbing the hollow cliff face, to the cave that like a dark socket bored a cavity, an orifice, half-way up the crag.

Before she could realize, her little bearers were staggering in the footholds, climbing the rock. She, too, was behind the ice. There it hung, like a curtain that is not spread, but hangs like a great fang. And near above her was the orifice of the cave sinking dark into the rock. She watched it as she swayed upwards.

On the platform of the cave stood the priests, waiting in all their gorgeousness of feathers and fringed robes, watching her ascent. Two of them stooped to help her litter-bearers. And at length she was on the platform of the cave, far in behind the shaft of ice, above the hollow amphitheatre among the bushes below, where men were dancing, and the whole population of the village was clustered in silence.

The sun was sloping down the afternoon sky, on the left. She knew that this was the shortest day of the year, and the last day of her life. They stood her facing the iridescent column of ice, which fell down marvellously arrested, away in front of her.

Some signal was given, and the dance below stopped. There was now absolute silence. She was given a little to drink, then two priests took off her mantle and her tunic, and in her strange pallor she stood there, between the lurid robes of the priests, beyond the pillar of ice, beyond and above the dark-faced people. The throng below gave a low, wild cry. Then the priests turned her round, so she stood with her back to the open world, her long blonde hair to the people below. And they cried again.

She was facing the cave, inwards. A fire was burning and flickering in the depths. Four priests had taken off their robes, and were almost as naked as she was. They were powerful men in the prime of life, and they kept their dark, painted faces lowered.

From the fire came the old, old priest, with an incense-pan. He was naked and in a state of barbaric ecstasy. He fumigated his victim, reciting at the same time in a hollow voice. Behind him came another robeless priest, with two flint knives.

When she was fumigated, they laid her on a large flat stone, the four powerful men holding her by the outstretched arms and legs. Behind stood the aged man, like a skeleton covered with dark glass, holding a knife and transfixedly watching the sun; and behind him again was another naked priest, with a knife.

She felt little sensation, though she knew all that was happening. Turning to the sky, she looked at the yellow sun. It was sinking. The shaft of ice was like a shadow between her and it. And she realized that the yellow rays were filling half the cave, though they had not reached the altar where the fire was, at the far end of the funnel-shaped cavity.

Yes, the rays were creeping round slowly. As they grew ruddier, they penetrated farther. When the red sun was about to sink, he would shine full through the shaft of ice deep into the hollow of the cave, to the innermost.

She understood now that this was what the men were waiting for. Even those that held her down were bent and twisted round, their black eyes watching the sun with a glittering eagerness, and awe, and craving. The black eyes of the aged cacique were fixed like black mirrors on the sun, as if sightless, yet containing some terrible answer to the reddening winter planet. And all the eyes of the priests were fixed and glittering on the sinking orb, in the reddening, icy silence of the winter afternoon.

They were anxious, terribly anxious, and fierce. Their ferocity wanted something, and they were waiting the moment. And their ferocity was ready to leap out into a mystic exultance, of triumph. But still they were anxious.

Only the eyes of that oldest man were not anxious. Black, and fixed, and as if sightless, they watched the sun, seeing beyond the sun. And in their black, empty concentration there was power, power intensely abstract and remote, but deep, deep to the heart of the earth, and the heart of the sun. In absolute motionlessness he watched till the red sun should send his ray through the column of ice. Then the old man would strike, and strike home, accomplish the sacrifice and achieve power.

The mastery that man must hold, and that passes from race to race.

Sun

'Take her away, into the sun,' the doctor said.

She herself was sceptical of the sun, but she permitted herself to be carried away, with her child, and a nurse, and her mother, over the sea.

The ship sailed at midnight. And for two hours her husband stayed with her, while the child was put to bed, and the passengers came on board. It was a black night, the Hudson swayed with heavy blackness, shaken over with spilled dribbles of light. She leaned on the rail, and looking down thought: This is the sea; it is deeper than one imagines, and fuller of memories. At that moment the sea seemed to heave like the serpent of chaos that has lived for ever.

'These partings are no good, you know,' her husband was saying, at her side. 'They're no good. I don't like them.'

His tone was full of apprehension, misgivings, and there was a certain note of clinging to the last straw of hope.

'No, neither do I,' she responded in a flat voice.

She remembered how bitterly they had wanted to get away from one another, he and she. The emotion of parting gave a slight tug at her emotions, but only caused the iron that had gone into her soul to gore deeper.

So, they looked at their sleeping son, and the father's eyes were wet. But it is not the wetting of the eyes which counts, it is the deep iron rhythm of habit, the year-long, lifelong habits; the deep-set stroke of power.

And in their two lives, the stroke of power was hostile, his and hers. Like two engines running at variance, they shattered one another.

'All ashore! All ashore!'

'Maurice, you must go!'

And she thought to herself: For him it is *All ashore!* For me it is *Out to sea!*

Well, he waved his hanky on the midnight dreariness of the pier, as the boat inched away; one among a crowd. One among a crowd! *C'est ça!*

The ferry-boats, like great dishes piled with rows of lights, were still slanting across the Hudson. That black mouth must be the Lackawanna Station.

The ship ebbed on, the Hudson seemed interminable. But at last they were round the bend, and there was the poor harvest of lights at the Battery. Liberty flung up her torch in a tantrum. There was the wash of the sea.

And though the Atlantic was grey as lava, she did come at last into the sun. Even she had a house above the bluest of seas, with a vast garden, or vineyard, all vines and olives dropping steeply, terrace after terrace, to the strip of coast-plain; and the garden full of secret places, deep groves of lemon far down in the cleft of earth, and hidden, pure green reservoirs of water; then a spring issuing out of a little cavern, where the old Sicules had drunk before the Greeks came; and a grey goat bleating, stabled in an ancient tomb, with all the niches empty. There was the scent of mimosa, and beyond, the snow of the volcano.

She saw it all, and in a measure it was soothing. But it was all external. She didn't really care about it. She was herself, just the same, with all her anger and frustration inside her, and her incapacity to feel anything real. The child irritated her, and preyed on her peace of mind. She felt so horribly, ghastly responsible for him: as if she must be responsible for every breath he drew. And that was torture to her, to the child, and to everybody else concerned.

'You know, Juliet, the doctor told you to lie in the sun, without your clothes. Why don't you?' said her mother.

'When I am fit to do so, I will. Do you want to kill me?' Juliet flew at her.

'To kill you, no! Only to do you good.'

'For God's sake, leave off wanting to do me good.'

The mother at last was so hurt and incensed, she departed.

The sea went white – and then invisible. Pouring rain fell. It was cold, in the house built for the sun.

Again a morning when the sun lifted himself naked and molten, sparkling over the sea's rim. The house faced south-west. Juliet lay in her bed and watched him rise. It was as if she had never seen the sun rise before. She had never seen the naked sun stand up pure upon the sea-line, shaking the night off himself.

So the desire sprang secretly in her, to go naked in the sun. She cherished her desire like a secret.

But she wanted to go away from the house – away from people. And it is not easy, in a country were every olive tree has eyes, and every slope is seen from afar, to go hidden.

But she found a place: a rocky bluff, shoved out to the sea and sun and overgrown with large cactus, the flat-leaved cactus called prickly pear. Out of this blue-grey knoll of cactus rose one cypress tree, with a pallid, thick trunk, and a tip that leaned over, flexible, up in the blue. It stood like a guardian looking to sea; or a low, silvery candle whose huge flame was darkness against light: earth sending up her proud tongue of gloom.

Juliet sat down by the cypress trees, and took off her clothes. The contorted cactus made a forest, hideous yet fascinating, about her. She sat and offered her bosom to the sun, sighing, even now, with a certain hard pain, against the cruelty of having to give herself.

But the sun marched in blue heaven and sent down his rays as he went. She felt the soft air of the sea on her breasts, that seemed as if they would never ripen. But she hardly felt the sun. Fruits that would wither and not mature, her breasts.

Soon, however, she felt the sun inside them, warmer than ever love had been, warmer than milk or the hands of her baby. At last, at last her breasts were like long white grapes in the hot sun.

She slid off all her clothes and lay naked in the sun, and as she lay she looked up through her fingers at the central sun, his blue pulsing round-ness, whose outer edges streamed brilliance. Pulsing with marvellous blue, and alive, and streaming white fire from his edges, the sun! He faced down to her with his look of blue fire, and enveloped her breasts and her face, her throat, her tired belly, her knees, her thighs and her feet.

She lay with shut eyes, the colour of rosy flame through her lids. It was too much. She reached and put leaves over her eyes. Then she lay again, like a long white gourd in the sun, that must ripen to gold.

She could feel the sun penetrating even into her bones; nay, further, even into her emotions and her thoughts. The dark tensions of her emotion began to give way, the cold dark clots of her thoughts began to dissolve. She was beginning to feel warm right through. Turning over, she let her shoulders dissolve in the sun, her loins, the backs of her thighs, even her heels. And she lay half stunned with wonder at the thing that was happening to her. Her weary, chilled heart was melting, and, in melting, evaporating.

When she was dressed again she lay once more and looked up at the cypress tree, whose crest, a flexible filament, fell this way and that in the breeze. Meanwhile, she was conscious of the great sun roaming in heaven.

So, dazed, she went home, only half-seeing, sunblinded and sun-dazed. And her blindness was like a richness to her, and her dim, warm, heavy half-consciousness was like wealth.

'Mummy! Mummy!' her child came running towards her, calling in that peculiar bird-like little anguish of want, always wanting her. She was surprised that her drowsed heart for once felt none of the anxious love-anguish in return. She caught the child up in her arms, but she thought: He should not be such a lump! If he were in the sun, he would spring up.

She resented, rather, his little hands clutching at her, especially at her neck. She pulled her throat away. She did not want to be touched. She put the child gently down.

'Run!' she said. 'Run in the sun!'

And there and then she took off his clothes and set him naked on the warm terrace.

'Play in the sun!' she said.

He was frightened and wanted to cry. But she, in the warm indolence of her body, and the complete indifference of her heart, rolled him an orange across the red tiles, and with his soft, unformed little body he toddled after it. Then immediately he had it he dropped it because it felt strange against his flesh. And he looked back at her, querulous, wrinkling his face to cry, frightened because he was stark.

'Bring me the orange,' she said, amazed at her own deep indifference to his trepidation. 'Bring Mummy the orange.'

'He shall not grow up like his father,' she said to herself. 'Like a worm that the sun has never seen.'

She had had the child so much on her mind, in a torment of responsibility, as if, having borne him, she had to answer for his whole existence. Even if his nose were running, it had been repulsive and a goad in her vitals, as if she must say to herself: Look at the thing you brought forth!

Now a change took place. She was no longer vitally interested in the child, she took the strain of her anxiety and her will from off him. And he thrived all the more for it.

She was thinking inside herself, of the sun in his splendour, and her mating with him. Her life was now a whole ritual. She lay always awake, before dawn, watching for the grey to colour to pale gold, to know if clouds lay on the sea's edge. Her joy was when he rose all molten in his nakedness, and threw off blue-white fire, into the tender heaven.

But sometimes he came ruddy, like a big, shy creature. And sometimes slow and crimson red, with a look of anger, slowly pushing and shouldering. Sometimes again she could not see him,

only the level cloud threw down gold and scarlet
from above, as he moved behind the wall.

She was fortunate. Weeks went by, and though
the dawn was sometimes clouded, and afternoon
was sometimes grey, never a day passed sunless,
and most days, winter though it was, streamed
radiant. The thin little wild crocuses came up
mauve and striped, the wild narcissi hung their
winter stars.

Every day she went down to the cypress tree,
among the cactus grove on the knoll with
yellowish cliffs at the foot. She was wiser and
subtler now, wearing only a dove-grey wrapper,
and sandals. So that in an instant, in any hidden
niche, she was naked to the sun. And the moment
she was covered again she was grey and invisible.

Every day, in the morning towards noon, she
lay at the foot of the powerful, silver-pawed
cypress tree, while the sun rode jovial in heaven. By now she knew the sun in every thread of
her body, there was not a cold shadow left. And
her heart, that anxious, straining heart had dis-
appeared altogether, like a flower that falls in the
sun, and leaves only a ripe seed-case.

She knew that sun in heaven, blue-molten
with his white fire edges, throwing off fire. And
though he shone on all the world, when she lay
unclothed he focused on her. It was one of the
wonders of the sun, he could shine on a million
people and still be the radiant, splendid, unique
sun, focused on her alone.

With her knowledge of the sun, and her

conviction that the sun *knew* her, in the cosmic carnal sense of the word, came over her a feeling of detachment from people, and a certain contempt for human beings altogether. They were so un-elemental, so unsunned. They were so like graveyard worms.

Even the peasants passing up the rocky, ancient little road with their donkeys, sun-blackened as they were, were not sunned right through. There was a little soft white core of fear, like a snail in a shell, where the soul of the man cowered in fear of death, and in fear of the natural blaze of life. He dared not quite emerge: always innerly cowed. All men were like that.

Why admit men!

With her indifference to people, to men, she was not now so cautious about being unseen. She had told Marinina, who went shopping for her in the village, that the doctor had ordered sunbaths. Let that suffice.

Marinina was a woman over sixty, tall, thin, erect, with curling dark grey hair, and dark grey eyes that had the shrewdness of thousands of years in them, with the laugh that underlies all long experience. Tragedy is lack of experience.

'It must be beautiful to go unclothed in the sun,' said Marinina, with a shrewd laugh in her eyes, as she looked keenly at the other woman. Juliet's fair, bobbed hair curled in a little cloud at her temple. Marinina was a woman of Magna Graecia, and had far memories. She looked again at Juliet. 'But you have to be beautiful yourself, if you're not going to give offence to the sun? Isn't it so?' she added, with that queer, breathless little laugh of the women of the past.

'Who knows if I am beautiful!' said Juliet.

But beautiful or not, she felt that by the sun she was appreciated. Which is the same.

When, out of the sun at noon, sometimes she stole down over the rocks and past the cliff-edge, down to the deep gully where the lemons hung in cool eternal shadow, and in the silence slipped off her wrapper to wash herself quickly at one of the deep, clear green basins, she would notice, in the bare green twilight under the lemon leaves, that all her body was rosy, rosy and turning to gold. She was like another person. She was another person.

So she remembered that the Greeks had said, a white, unsunned body was fishy and unhealthy.

And she would rub a little olive oil in her skin, and wander a moment in the dark underworld of the lemons, balancing a lemon flower in her navel, laughing to herself. There was just a chance some peasant might see her. But if he did he would be more afraid of her than she of him. She knew the white core of fear in the clothed bodies of men.

She knew it even in her little son. How he mistrusted her, now that she laughed at him, with the sun in her face! She insisted on his toddling naked in the sunshine, every day. And now his little body was pink, too, his blond hair was pushed thick from his brow, his cheeks had a

pomegranate scarlet, in the delicate gold of the
sunny skin. He was bonny and healthy, and the
servants, loving his red and gold and blue, called
him an angel from heaven.

But he mistrusted his mother: she laughed at
him. And she saw in his wide blue eyes, under the
little frown, that centre of fear, misgiving, which
she believed was at the centre of all male eyes,
now. She called it fear of the sun.

'He fears the sun,' she would say to herself,
looking down into the eyes of the child.

And as she watched him toddling, swaying,
tumbling in the sunshine, making his little, bird-
like noises, she saw that he held himself tight and
hidden from the sun, inside himself. His spirit was
like a snail in a shell, in a damp, cold crevice inside
himself. It made her think of his father. She
wished she could make him come forth, break
out in a gesture of recklessness and salutation.

She determined to take him with her, down to
the cypress tree among the cactus. She would
have to watch him, because of the thorns. But
surely in that place he would come forth from that
little shell, deep inside him. That little civilized
tension would disappear off his brow.

She spread a rug for him and sat him down.
Then she slid off her wrapper and lay down
herself, watching a hawk high in the blue, and
the tip of the cypress hanging over.

The boy played with stones on the rug. When
he got up to toddle away, she sat up too. He
turned and looked at her. Almost, from his blue

eyes, it was the challenging, warm look of the true male. And he was handsome, with the scarlet in the golden blond of his skin. He was not really white. His skin was gold-dusky.

'Mind the thorns, darling,' she said.

'Thorns!' re-echoed the child, in a birdy chirp, still looking at her over his shoulder, like some naked cherub in a picture, doubtful.

'Nasty prickly thorns.'

''Ickly thorns!'

He staggered in his little sandals over the stones, pulling at the dry wild mint. She was quick as a serpent, leaping to him, when he was going to fall against the prickles. It surprised even herself. 'What a wild cat I am, really!' she said to herself.

She brought him every day, when the sun shone, to the cypress tree.

'Come!' she said. 'Let us go to the cypress tree.'

And if there was a cloudy day, with the tramontana blowing, so that she could not go down, the child would chirp incessantly: 'Cypress tree! Cypress tree!'

He missed it as much as she did.

It was not just taking sunbaths. It was much more than that. Something deep inside her unfolded and relaxed, and she was given. By some mysterious power inside her, deeper than her known consciousness and will, she was put into connection with the sun, and the stream flowed of itself, from her womb. She herself, her conscious self, was secondary, a secondary person,

almost an onlooker. The true Juliet was this dark
flow from her deep body to the sun.

She had always been mistress of herself, aware
of what she was doing, and held tense for her own
power. Now she felt inside her quite another sort
of power, something greater than herself, flowing
by itself. Now she was vague, but she had a power
beyond herself.

The end of February was suddenly very hot.
Almond blossom was falling like pink snow, in
the touch of the smallest breeze. The mauve, silky
little anemones were out, the asphodels tall in
bud; and the sea was cornflower blue.

Juliet had ceased to trouble about anything.
Now, most of the day, she and the child were
naked in the sun, and it was all she wanted.
Sometimes she went down to the sea to bathe:
often she wandered in the gullies where the sun
shone in, and she was out of sight. Sometimes
she saw a peasant with an ass, and he saw her.
But she went so simply and quietly with her
child; and the fame of the sun's healing power,
for the soul as well as for the body, had already
spread among the people; so that there was no
excitement.

The child and she were now both tanned with
a rosy-golden tan, all over. 'I am another being!'
she said to herself, as she looked at her red-gold
breasts and thighs.

The child, too, was another creature, with a
peculiar quiet, sun-darkened absorption. Now he

played by himself in silence, and she hardly need notice him. He seemed no longer to know when he was alone.

There was not a breeze, and the sea was ultramarine. She sat by the great silver paw of the cypress tree, drowsed in the sun, but her breasts alert, full of sap. She was becoming aware that an activity was rousing in her, an activity which would carry her into a new way of life. Still she did not want to be aware. She knew well enough the vast cold apparatus of civilization, so difficult to evade.

The child had gone a few yards down the rocky path, round the great sprawling of a cactus. She had seen him, a real gold-brown infant of the winds, with burnt gold hair and red cheeks, collecting the speckled pitcher-flowers and laying them in rows. He could balance now, and was quick for his own emergencies, like an absorbed young animal playing silent.

Suddenly she heard him speaking: '*Look, Mummy! Mummy, look!*' A note in his bird-like voice made her lean forward sharply.

Her heart stood still. He was looking over his naked little shoulder at her, and pointing with a loose little hand at a snake which had reared itself up a yard away from him, and was opening its mouth so that its forked, soft tongue flickered back like a shadow, uttering a short hiss.

'Look, Mummy!'

'Yes, darling, it's a snake!' came the slow, deep voice.

He looked at her, his wide blue eyes uncertain whether to be afraid or not. Some stillness of the sun in her reassured him.

'Snake!' he chirped.

'Yes, darling! Don't touch it, it can bite.'

The snake had sunk down, and was reaching away from the coils in which it had been basking asleep, and slowly was easing its long, gold-brown body into the rocks, with slow curves. The boy turned and watched it in silence. Then he said:

'Snake going!'

'Yes! Let it go. It likes to be alone.'

He still watched the slow, easing length as the creature drew itself apathetic out of sight.

'Snake gone back,' he said.

'Yes, it's gone back. Come to Mummy a moment.'

He came and sat with his plump, naked little body on her naked lap, and she smoothed his burnt, bright hair. She said nothing, feeling that everything was passed. The curious soothing power of the sun filled her, filled the whole place like a charm, and the snake was part of the place, along with her and the child.

Another day, in the dry stone wall of one of the olive terraces, she saw a black snake horizontally creeping.

'Marinina,' she said, 'I saw a black snake. Are they harmful?'

'Ah, the black snakes, no! But the yellow ones, yes! If the yellow one bite you, you die. But they frighten me, they frighten me, even the black ones, when I see one.'

Juliet still went to the cypress tree with the child. But she always looked carefully round before she sat down, examining everywhere where the child might go. Then she would lie and turn to the sun again, her tanned, pear-shaped breasts pointing up. She would take no thought for the morrow. She refused to think outside her garden, and she could not write letters. She would tell the nurse to write.

It was March, and the sun was growing very powerful. In the hot hours she would lie in the shade of the trees, or she would even go down to the depths of the cool lemon grove. The child ran in the distance, like a young animal absorbed in life.

One day she was sitting in the sun on the steep slope of the gully, having bathed in one of the great tanks. Below, under the lemons, the child was wading among the yellow oxalis flowers of the shadow, gathering fallen lemons, passing with his tanned little body into flecks of light, moving all dappled.

Suddenly, high over the land's edge, against the full-lit pale blue sky, Marinina appeared, a black cloth tied round her head, calling quietly: '*Signora! Signora Giulietta!*'

Juliet faced round, standing up. Marinina paused a moment, seeing the naked woman standing alert, her sun-faded fair hair in a little

cloud. Then the swift old woman came on down
the slant of the steep track.

She stood a few steps, erect, in front of the sun-
coloured woman, and eyed her shrewdly.

'But how beautiful you are, you!' she said
coolly, almost cynically. 'There is your husband.'

'My husband!' cried Juliet.

The old woman gave a shrewd bark of a little
laugh, the mockery of the women of the past.

'Haven't you got one, a husband, you?' she
taunted.

'But where is he?' cried Juliet.

The old woman glanced over her shoulder.

'He was following me,' she said. 'But he will
not have found the path.' And she gave another
little bark of a laugh.

The paths were all grown high with grass and
flowers and nepitella, till they were like bird-trails
in an eternally wild place. Strange, the vivid
wildness of the old places of civilization, a wildness that is not gaunt.

Juliet looked at her serving-woman with
meditating eyes.

'Oh, very well!' she said at last. 'Let him come.'

'Let him come here? Now?' asked Marinina,
her laughing, smoke-grey eyes looking with
mockery into Juliet's. Then she gave a little jerk
of her shoulders.

'All right, as you wish. But for him it is a rare
one!'

She opened her mouth in a laugh of noiseless
joy. Then she pointed down to the child, who

was heaping lemons against his little chest. 'Look how beautiful the child is! That, certainly, will please him, poor thing. Then I'll bring him.'

'Bring him,' said Juliet.

The old woman scrambled rapidly up the track again. Maurice was standing grey-faced, in his grey felt hat and his dark grey suit, at a loss among the vine terraces. He looked pathetically out of place, in that resplendent sunshine and the grace of the old Greek world; like a blot of ink on the pale, sun-glowing slope.

'Come!' said Marinina to him. 'She is down here.'

And swiftly she led the way, striding with a rapid stride, making her way through the grasses. Suddenly she stopped on the brow of the slope. The tops of the lemon trees were dark, away below.

'You, you go down here,' she said to him, and he thanked her, looking up at her swiftly.

He was a man of forty, clean-shaven, grey-faced, very quiet and really shy. He managed his own business carefully, without startling success, but efficiently. And he confided in nobody. The old woman of Magna Graecia saw him at a glance: he is good, she said to herself, but not a man, poor thing.

'Down there is the Signora!' said Marinina, pointing like one of the Fates.

And again he said 'Thank you! Thank you!' without a twinkle, and stepped carefully into the track. Marinina lifted her chin with a joyful wickedness. Then she strode off towards the house.

Maurice was watching his step, through the tangle of Mediterranean herbage, so he did not catch sight of his wife till he came round a little bend, quite near her. She was standing erect and nude by the jutting rock, glistening with the sun and with warm life. Her breasts seemed to be lifting up, alert, to listen, her thighs looked brown and fleet. Her glance on him, as he came like ink on blotting-paper, was swift and nervous.

Maurice, poor fellow, hesitated, and glanced away from her. He turned his face aside.

'Hello, Julie!' he said, with a little nervous cough – 'Splendid! Splendid!'

He advanced with his face averted, shooting further glances at her, as she stood with the peculiar satiny gleam of the sun on her tanned skin. Somehow she did not seem so terribly naked. It was the golden-rose tan of the sun that clothed her.

'Hello, Maurice!' she said, hanging back from him. 'I wasn't expecting you so soon.'

'No,' he said, 'No! I managed to slip away a little earlier.'

And again he coughed awkwardly.

They stood several yards away from one another, and there was silence.

'Well!' he said, 'er – this is splendid, splendid! You are – er – splendid! Where is the boy?'

'There he is,' she said, pointing down to where a naked urchin in the deep shade was piling fallen lemons together.

The father gave an odd little laugh.

'Ah, yes! There he is! So there's the little man! Fine!' he said. He really was thrilled in his suppressed, nervous soul. 'Hello, Johnny!' he called, and it sounded rather feeble. 'Hello, Johnny!'

The child looked up, spilling lemons from his chubby arms, but did not respond.

'I guess we'll go down to him,' said Juliet, as she turned and went striding down the path. Her husband followed, watching the rosy, fleet-looking lifting and sinking of her quick hips, as she swayed a little in the socket of her waist. He was dazed with admiration, but also, at a deadly loss. What should he do with himself? He was utterly out of the picture, in his dark grey suit and pale grey hat, and his grey monastic face of a shy business man.

'He looks all right, doesn't he,' said Juliet, as they came through the deep sea of yellow-flowering oxalis, under the lemon trees.

'Ah! – yes! yes! Splendid! Splendid! – Hello, Johnny! Do you know Daddy? Do you know Daddy, Johnny?'

He crouched down and held out his hands.

'Lemons!' said the child, birdily chirping. 'Two lemons!'

'Two lemons!' replied the father. 'Lots of lemons.'

The infant came and put a lemon in each of his father's open hands. Then he stood back to look.

'Two lemons!' repeated the father. 'Come, Johnny! Come and say "Hello" to Daddy.'

'Daddy going back?' said the child.

'Going back? Well – well – not today.'

And he gathered his son in his arms.

'Take a coat off! Daddy take a coat off!' said the boy, squirming debonair away from the cloth.

'All right, son! Daddy take a coat off.'

He took off his coat and laid it carefully aside, then again took his son in his arms. The naked woman looked down at the naked infant in the arms of the man in his shirt sleeves. The boy had pulled off the father's hat, and Juliet looked at the sleek, black-and-grey hair of her husband, not a hair out of place. And utterly, utterly indoors. She was silent for a long time, while the father talked to the child, who was fond of his Daddy.

'What are you going to do about it, Maurice?' she said, suddenly.

He looked at her swiftly, sideways.

'Er – about what, Julie?'

'Oh, everything! About this! I can't go back into East Forty-Seventh.'

'Er – ' he hesitated, 'no, I suppose not – not just now at least.'

'Never,' she said, and there was a silence.

'Well – er – I don't know,' he said.

'Do you think you can come out here?' she said.

'Yes! – I can stay for a month. I think I can manage a month,' he hesitated. Then he ventured a complicated, shy peep at her, and hid his face again.

She looked down at him, her alert breasts lifted with a sigh, as if a breeze of impatience shook them.

'I can't go back,' she said slowly. 'I can't go back on this sun. If you can't come here—'

She ended on an open note. He glanced at her again and again, furtively, but with growing admiration and lessening of confusion.

'No!' he said. 'This kind of thing suits you. You are splendid! No, I don't think you can go back.'

He was thinking of her in the New York flat, pale, silent, oppressing him terribly. He was the soul of gentle timidity, in his human relations, and her silent, awful hostility after the baby was born, had frightened him deeply. Because he had realized she couldn't help it. Women were like that. Their feelings took a reverse direction, even against their own selves, and it was awful – awful! Awful, awful to live in the house with a woman like that, whose feelings were reversed even against herself! He had felt himself ground down under the millstone of her helpless enmity. She had ground even herself down to the quick, and the child as well. No, anything rather than that.

'But what about *you?*' she asked.

'I? Oh, I! – I can carry on the business, and – er – come over here for the holidays – as long as you like to stay. You stay as long as you wish.' He looked a long time down at the earth, then glanced up at her with a touch of supplication in his uneasy eyes.

'Even for ever?'

'Well – er – yes, if you like. For ever is a long time. One can't set a date.'

'And I can do anything I like?' She looked him straight in the eyes, challenging. And he was powerless against her rosy, wind-hardened nakedness.

'Er – yes! – I suppose so! So long as you don't make yourself unhappy – or the boy.'

Again he looked up at her with a complicated, uneasy appeal – thinking of the child, but hoping for himself.

'I won't,' she said quickly.

'No!' he said. 'No! I don't think you will.'

There was a pause. The bells of the village were hastily clanging midday. That meant lunch.

She slipped into her grey crepe kimono, and fastened the broad green sash round her waist. Then she slipped a little blue shirt over the boy's head, and they went up to the house.

At table she watched her husband, his grey city face, his fixed, black-grey hair, his very precise table manners, and his extreme moderation in eating and drinking. Sometimes he glanced at her, furtively, from under his black lashes. He had the gold-grey eyes of an animal that has been caught young, and reared completely in captivity.

They went on to the balcony for coffee. Below, beyond, on the next podere across the steep little gully, a peasant and his wife were sitting under an almond tree, near the green wheat, eating their midday meal from a little white cloth spread on the ground. There was a huge piece of bread, and glasses with dark wine.

Juliet put her husband with his back to this picture; she sat facing. Because, the moment she and Maurice had come out on the balcony, the peasant had glanced up.

She knew him, in the distance, perfectly. He was a rather fat, very broad fellow of about thirty-five, and he chewed large mouthfuls of bread. His wife was stiff and dark-faced, handsome, sombre. They had no children. So much Juliet had learned.

The peasant worked a great deal alone, on the opposite podere. His clothes were always very clean and cared for, white trousers and a coloured shirt, and an old straw hat. Both he and his wife had that air of quiet superiority which belongs to individuals, not to a class.

His attraction was in his vitality, the peculiar quick energy which gave a charm to his movements, stout and broad as he was. In the early days before she took to the sun, Juliet had met him suddenly, among the rocks, when she had scrambled over to the next podere. He had been aware of her before she saw him, so that when she did look up, he took off his hat, gazing at her with shyness and pride, from his big blue eyes. His face was broad, sunburnt, he had a cropped brown moustache, and thick brown eyebrows, nearly as thick as his moustache, meeting under his low, wide brow.

'Oh!' she said. 'Can I walk here?'

'Surely!' he replied, with that peculiar hot haste which characterized his movement. 'My *padrone* would wish you to walk wherever you like on his land.'

And he pressed back his head in the quick, vivid, shy generosity of his nature. She had gone on quickly. But instantly she had recognized the violent generosity of his blood, and the equally violent *farouche* shyness.

Since then she had seen him in the distance every day, and she came to realize that he was one who lived a good deal to himself, like a quick animal, and that his wife loved him intensely, with a jealousy that was almost hate; because, probably, he wanted to give himself still, still further, beyond where she could take him.

One day, when a group of peasants sat under a tree, she had seen him dancing quick and gay with a child – his wife watching darkly.

Gradually Juliet and he had become intimate, across the distance. They were aware of one another. She knew, in the morning, the moment he arrived with his ass. And the moment she went out on the balcony he turned to look. But they never saluted. Yet she missed him when he did not come to work on the podere.

Once, in the hot morning when she had been walking naked, in the gully between the two estates, she had come upon him, as he was bending down, with his powerful shoulders, picking up wood to pile on his motionless, waiting donkey. He saw her as he lifted his flushed face, and she was backing away. A flame went over his eyes, and a flame flew over her body, melting her bones. But she backed away behind the bushes, silently, and retreated whence she had come. And she wondered a little resentfully over the silence in which he could work, hidden in the bushy places. He had that wild animal faculty.

Since then there had been a definite pain of consciousness in the body of each of them, though neither would admit it, and they gave no sign of recognition. But the man's wife was instinctively aware.

And Juliet had thought: Why shouldn't I meet this man for an hour, and bear his child? Why should I have to identify my life with a man's life? Why not meet him for an hour, as long as the desire lasts, and no more? There is already the spark between us.

But she had never made any sign. And now she saw him looking up, from where he sat by the white cloth, opposite his black-clad wife, looking up at Maurice. The wife turned and looked, too, saturnine.

And Juliet felt a grudge come over her. She would have to bear Maurice's child again. She had seen it in her husband's eyes. And she knew it from his answer, when she spoke to him.

'Will you walk about in the sun, too, without your clothes?' she asked him.

'Why – er – yes! Yes, I should like to, while I'm here – I suppose it's quite private?'

There was a gleam in his eyes, a desperate kind

of courage of his desire, and a glance at the alert lifting of her breasts in her wrapper. In this way, he was a man, too, he faced the world and was not entirely quenched in his male courage. He would dare to walk in the sun, even ridiculously.

But he smelled of the world, and all its fetters and its mongrel cowering. He was branded with the brand that is not a hallmark.

Ripe now, and brown-rosy all over with the sun, and with a heart like a fallen rose, she had wanted to go down to the hot, shy peasant and bear his child. Her sentiments had fallen like petals. She had seen the flushed blood in the burnt face, and the flame in the southern blue eyes, and the answer in her had been a gush of fire. He would have been a procreative sunbath to her, and she wanted it.

Nevertheless, her next child would be Maurice's. The fatal chain of continuity would cause it.